Twisted Memories

Twisted Memories

Rebecca Rose

WINTERFIELD PRESS

Copyright © 2016 by Rebecca Rose
ISBN-10: 0-9911185-2-9
ISBN-13: 978-0-9911185-2-6

To Laura.

If not for you there would be no me, the author. Some say angels are put in our lives to guide us places we couldn't find on our own. You will always be that for me.

Chapter One

It's been almost three months now since I've slept a whole night through. I've been haunted by a nightmare of my mother's death. The dream is the same every night; I'm seven years old, asleep in the back seat of our station wagon. My mother is driving and it's night time. Suddenly I hear the tires squealing and when I open my eyes I see my mother looking back at me over the seat, desperately reaching for me; but she disappears. Then I wake up.

I opened my eyes and turned my head to the clock. 4.27 a.m. I squeezed my eyes shut and rolled over, a fistful of the covers in my hand, and adjusted my head on the pillow until it was just right. I took a big breath in and let it out slowly, knowing I had plenty of time before the alarm went off. You're fine Jen, just relax and go back to sleep. I tried to picture myself walking down the beach, waves crashing, spilling over my feet, hoping that would quiet my mind. I imagined the squawk of seagulls as they flew overhead. I searched for sea shells but suddenly the shells turned into files and I was at my desk flipping through papers. Oh, who was I kidding? I slapped the covers off and got out of bed, crossed over to the window and pulled open the blind. It was dark outside and quiet. Very soon the city would be bustling and people would be going about their everyday lives. My life revolved around work. I had no family, or at least that's how it felt.

I walked into the bathroom and flicked on the light. Cringing at the brightness until my eyes adjusted, I leaned on the counter and looked at myself in the mirror. My light brown hair spilled down over my shoulders as I leaned in closer. My mother's green eyes were staring back at me. I had many of her soft, feminine features; her high cheek bones and thin frame, despite my lack of exercise. But I was beginning to look old; old before my time. I was only twenty-nine; I shouldn't have bags under my eyes and pale skin. A few more years and I'd be thirty-three; the age my mother had been when she died.

I took a shower and got dressed for work. In the kitchen, I flicked on the TV, letting the news channel play in the background while I made coffee.

"Another shooting was reported at the East River last night. Police say drug activity at the sight has been an ongoing issue for over a year. Speculation is Vance Wallace is the suspect in this most recent shooting, but there is no evidence for arrest at this time. Up next, the forecast with John Fitzgerald."

Same, same, same; everything was still the same. I heard the neighbor across the hall leave right on schedule, whistling to his German shepherd. Maybe I should get a dog.

The shiny black Towne car was ready and waiting outside like always. I slid in, hearing the soft leather groan beneath me as I pulled the door closed.

"Good morning Ms. Callahan."

"Good morning Sam," I replied, feigning enthusiasm.

Sam slowly pulled away from the curb and out into the traffic. He was always chipper and happy. He had been my driver for the past four years and I had begun to notice that his hair was flecked with gray. He had driven my father for many years before he'd become my driver - I'd told my father it wasn't necessary, that I could drive myself or even take a cab to work. But there was no arguing with my father; there never was. He was supposedly retired, which was why Sam had taken on the responsibility of driving me. Unfortunately my father still made frequent appearances in the office.

"How are you today?" I asked.

"Oh, just fine thanks. I heard on the radio this morning there's going to be a big storm this weekend."

"That figures," I said under my breath. I picked up the newspaper and began thumbing through.

"Usual stop this morning?" Sam asked, peeking at me in the rear view mirror.

"Usual stop Sam," I said, without looking up.

We rode in silence until we reached my favorite coffee house. I loved the smell of the place, especially first thing in the morning; warm pastry and vanilla mixed with cinnamon. The sounds of whooshing steam and clinking dishes enveloped me and my tension melted away.

"Hey Jen, and how are you this fine morning?"

Eli was in college, and was always happy to see me. He made a mean mocha too. I secretly looked forward to his flirting because it made me feel young again - I even forget for a short while how boring shit was.

"Hey Eli. I'm fine. Do you ever have a day off, or do you live here?"

"I should just set up a bed out back and get it over with. It would save some time. Keeping our streets safe again today?"

I stiffened at the reminder of work. I'd been working for my father's law firm for almost four years as a defense attorney and the monotony of it all had been weighing on me. The need for something different, something new, something exciting, had been gnawing at me for a while now. "I wouldn't exactly call it that."

"Well, you coming in here every day makes what I do worth it." He handed me my coffee with a wink.

"Thank you Eli, that's nice of you to say. I'll see you tomorrow."

I took a sip of my mocha and swallowed it with my eyes closed, pleased with the creamy chocolate taste. Perfect as usual. Back in the car I gazed out the window as Sam drove me to my office.

I sighed as I watched the world passing by. Everything was the same; the traffic, the news, the people. And of course John. We turned a corner and there he was - sitting on his bench as always. John Doe, as I'd nicknamed him, had been sitting on that same bench across the street from my office building for the past eight months. But who was he? Why did he sit day after day staring at the court house?

Sam pulled the car to a stop.

"Have a good day Ms. Callahan. I'll see you this evening," he said with a smile.

❦

I stepped out of the elevator on the twelfth floor and into the reception area of Monroe, Lambert and Tate. My father had started the company right after he graduated law school and had made it successful. I grew up not wanting for anything. The only problem was, he was never around to be a father.

I walked up to the reception desk and heard Hall and Oates playing on the radio next to the phone. They were singing about someone making their dreams come true. I know what you mean.

"Good morning Rosemarie, any mail?"

Rosemarie was in her mid-fifties and had been working in reception since I could remember. She swayed to the beat of Hall and Oates, her long black skirt swirling round her ankles as she put papers in the employee mailboxes. She looked over her shoulder to greet me.

"Good morning Miss Callahan. Just some office memos is all." She handed me a pile.

"Oh goodie, thanks."

I'm not sure she even heard me because she was already back to swaying again, this time to the Bee Gee's 'Staying Alive.'

❧

Another week went by just like any other; busy and uninteresting. I was in court a lot - that used to be my favorite part of being a lawyer; arguing sides and winning, especially when it was against a male DA. My adrenaline kept me going, keeping me high and exhilarated, looking forward to my next win. Not a lot of women lawyers had the confidence I did in the court room. I got that from my father. He commanded respect with just his presence.

It was a new Monday morning and I knew everybody would be extra stressed. My father was returning from California. Although it was still early and the office was quiet, it was going to get busy soon and I wanted to soak in the peace while I had the chance.

I began thinking about my father. When my mother had died he'd sent me off to private school. It had felt like he was getting rid of me. I was so young; I didn't understand why my mother was gone and why I had to leave our home. I hated every minute of school but I did what I was told like a good little girl.

A flash of lightening brought me back to the present and the unexpected boom of thunder made me flinch. The weekend's storm wasn't over yet then. When the rain began I looked out the window at John. Sure enough he was prepared; he'd put up the large golf umbrella he'd had lying beneath his feet. He was moving over to make room for the woman next to him, making a gesture for her to share his umbrella. She sat closer, hugging her purse to her chest.

He was dressed differently, in khaki pants and a collared shirt. He still had his old backpack with him though. Maybe he was going somewhere today. Or maybe someone was meeting him and he wanted to look nice. Job interview? He had to have a home; I couldn't imagine those clothes looking like that after being in a backpack. I wondered why I even cared.

I sat for a while and watched as they talked. John seemed unconcerned that his feet were getting wet as the rain increased and cars whizzed by spraying water from their tires. The thunder was loud and every time the woman next to him heard it she would hunch her shoulders, looking scared, her eyes wide. John inched closer to her and the woman smiled. He seemed confident but his posture was stiff and he didn't look at her much. They talked for a while until the bus came and they both stood up. The woman got on but John went back to the bench and sat down. That was so sweet of him to make sure she stayed dry, but why didn't he get on the bus? Why didn't he ever go anywhere?

The moment ended when my assistant Karen came in.

She jumped a little to see me already at my desk. "Oh, you're in early."

She'd been my assistant since I'd started working for my father. I'd interviewed and hired her myself. She was a hard worker and had proven to be a great asset to me. Her long legs looked great in her grey pencil skirt.

"Good morning Karen. Those aren't for me, are they?"

She looked at her arms, full of files, then back to me with a smile. "No, just putting these away. How come you're here so early? Your calendar's clear this morning."

"My father will be back today so I just wanted to make sure I had everything in order. You didn't see him when you came in, did you?" My heart leapt into my throat.

"No, his office was still closed when I came in. Do you want me to let you know when he's here?"

I let out a sigh of relief. "Yes, I'd appreciate that," I said trying to hide the dread in my voice. "Can you close my door when you leave please? Thanks Karen."

❦

Just after eleven my intercom came on.

"Ms. Callahan, your father just came in."

"Thanks Karen."

I was surprised at the late hour, but he was the boss and didn't have anyone to answer to. I decided to greet him before he had a chance to come and check up on me.

He was standing behind his desk shuffling through a stack of messages. It never ceased to amaze me how, even at the age of seventy-four, he was still very handsome. He was wearing a dark blue suit with a red tie, looking sophisticated and domineering as always. His grey hair was combed to perfection. The light from his desk lamp reflected on his gold wedding ring, catching my eye. Why did he still wear that? Would I ever understand this man?

My heart was beating in my ears and my hands were clammy. Jesus Jennifer, get ahold of yourself. I pushed my shoulders back.

"Hello Daddy, how was your trip?"

He looked up at me and smiled. "Hello, it's good to see you. I assume all remains in tack around here?"

I kissed him lightly on the cheek. He smelled of his usual crisp aftershave.

"Of course," I said, forcing a laugh. "How are things in California?"

"Hot. But our clients are happy again and all is good with the world."

"Well, I just wanted to welcome you back. I've got work to do so I'll let you get settled back in."

"We'll have dinner this week."

"Sure," I said dryly. He wasn't expecting me to answer him anyway. I turned on my heel and walked out of his office - he was already making a phone call. I missed you too, Dad.

Chapter Two

It was pouring when I left that evening. My mood had gone from bored to bad after seeing my father. The two of us had never been close and it bothered me that I felt more like an employee than a daughter. I missed my mother more on days like this.

It rained more often than not in New York City, especially after the winter season. Now that spring was turning into summer I had been looking forward to longer days and warmer weather. Although I had been raised here and I loved the city, I'd also always shared my mother's love for the beach.

When I saw my car lined up with all the others at the curb, I ran quickly in a sorry attempt not to get wet. That didn't work.

"I didn't see you coming Ms. Callahan, otherwise I would have met you with the umbrella," Sam said, watching me from the front seat as I scurried into the car.

"That's okay, Sam, I won't melt." I smiled reassuringly.

We hadn't gone far when I heard a loud bang; it sounded almost like a gun shot. The car swerved to the left and Sam jerked it back to the right. We slowly came to a stop along the curb as I heard the flopping thud of what I assumed to be a flat tire. I was instantly irritated. It seemed as if the universe was playing a sick joke on me and wouldn't let my bad day come to an end.

"What happened, Sam?"

"We have a flat. I'm going to have to call Triple A," he said, fumbling with his phone. "Would you like me to hail you a cab first?"

Shit! I looked out the window and shook my head in disbelief. "No, there won't be any cabs available in this weather." I sat back in the seat as my irritation ignited like a fire. I probably wouldn't have been so mad had my father still been out of town. Whenever I saw him it was as if nothing went right. I rubbed at my forehead, trying to keep a headache at bay. Suddenly craving coffee, I looked up and saw a diner a couple of doors away. "I'm gonna go over to that diner and get some coffee. You want me to bring you some?"

"No thanks," he replied, tapping his watch. "It's after five."

"Suit yourself. I'll just wait in there then. Let me know when the car's ready."

I grabbed Sam's umbrella from the front seat and got out of the car as sheets of rain came down from every direction. I ran to the door and made my way into the quiet diner, hearing a little bell ring above me as the door opened and closed. The only people in the diner were a man in a booth, a waitress and the cook. I could hear seventies soft rock playing lightly as I dripped my way over to the counter. My wet skin turned to goose bumps as the air conditioning hit me.

"Can I get you something warm?" the waitress asked. She was wearing a light brown dress with a white collar and white cuffed sleeves. There was what looked like a folded up doily and a nametag on the front of her dress that read 'Gerry.' Was I in a time warp or something? Between the music and Gerry's outfit I expected Flo to come out and tell me to kiss her grits.

"Yes, just coffee please," I said, dropping the umbrella and brushing rain from my lap. I shook my hands at my side and reached for some napkins. Shit, the holder was empty. I turned around to retrieve one from a table behind me and caught sight of the man sitting in the booth. It was John Doe. I had never seen him anywhere else but on the bench outside my office. My heart started to beat faster and I realized I was nervous; this was the most exciting thing that had happened in my boring life lately. He was eating a plate of pancakes and bacon and there was a cup of coffee in front of him. He didn't look up.

The waitress came with my coffee.

"Can I get 'cha anything else?" she asked.

I turned around and sat down on a circular stool, practically spinning off it as I tried to act cool. "No, thank you."

I looked over my shoulder. John didn't seem to have noticed that I was making a complete fool out of myself. I turned back to my coffee and added some cream and sugar. My hands were still wet but I didn't really care anymore.

I sat there stirring my coffee wondering if I should say something. What would I say though? He had no idea who I was. What reason could I possibly have for needing to talk to him? As I drank my coffee I realized I wasn't pissed any more or stressed about my father. In fact I felt excited and filled with adrenaline at the thought of possibly finding out the mystery behind the man on the bench. My curiosity about him was piqued. My father used to tell me: "Every client will lie and they will always have a story. It is up to you to find out the truth." But John wasn't a client and his story was none of my business.

I turned and looked over my shoulder again, unable to contain my curiosity about him. He looked like he was almost finished with his pancakes. He put his fork down and reached for a napkin and wiped his mouth. He shuffled around with his backpack briefly, and I hoped he wasn't getting ready to leave. He looked up, searching for the waitress and our eyes met. Holy shit, he was gorgeous! His hair was brown and thick, curling around the back of his neck. He beamed at me and I felt my cheeks warm. I was struck by the blue color of his eyes; there was an unusual hint of brown in his left eye. His face was covered with a dusting of stubble, filling in, but not hiding, the cleft on his chin. And his lips…oh, his lips were full and divine. My breathing quickened as my imagination went into overdrive, wondering what those lips would feel like on my neck. I watched as the corners of his mouth turned up into a smile. You're staring, you idiot.

The waitress interrupted our staring contest, blocking my view. I turned back to my coffee, my stomach tied up in knots wondering what he was thinking. Probably thinking that I was a lunatic!

"Are you all finished honey?" Gerry asked John. "Here's your check, I'll be back in a minute. Would you like me to top off that coffee?"

"Yes, thank you," John said in a low, deep voice.

"Alright then, be right back. How 'bout you honey? Would you like a topper?"

I turned to see the waitress holding the pot in the air and John looking into his cup.

"Sure," I said.

"It doesn't look like that rain will ever let up. Are you sure you don't want something to eat?"

"Oh, no thank you. I won't be here much longer."

"Alrighty then, you just let me know." She walked away.

I added more cream and sugar to my fresh cup of coffee. I wondered if Triple A had arrived yet. I should probably go check on Sam; I'd left him out there all by himself.

"Excuse me."

My stomach tied one knot tighter. I turned around to see John looking at me. My heart was pounding.

"I'm out of cream here. You think I could borrow yours?"

"Oh…of course….here." I stood up and took the cream jug to his table.

"Thank you, I appreciate that," he said, pouring a small amount into his mug.

Like a dummy I remained standing at his table, unable to move. I felt as though I was trying to help a stray dog but I wasn't sure if he was going to bite me or not.

"This rain is really something today, huh?"

He nodded his head impassively.

I looked around the diner, searching my brain for something else to say. What was wrong with me? If I were in court and he was a witness I would have found a way to get him to answer me.

"My name is Jennifer by the way," I said, putting a hand out.

"Lucas. It's nice to meet you," he said, returning my gesture. We shook hands lightly, my grip tighter than his. "Would you like to sit down?"

Hell yes, I wanted to sit down. I guess the stray dog trusted me after all. "Sure." I turned and picked up my mug from the counter and returned to the booth, sitting across from him. "Do you come here a lot? Is it always this slow?"

"I come a few times a week. It's busiest at lunch time. They have great pancakes."

"I'm not used to being in such a quiet place like this. It's a bit unnerving actually."

"So what brings you in today?"

"My car has a flat tire. I came in to wait for Triple A. I work just around the corner. At Monroe, Lambert and Tate."

"Are you an attorney?"

"Ah…yes, I am," I said. Work was not the subject I wanted to be talking about. It was the only thing I had to show for my life; but it was the one thing I resented lately. I had no husband, no children, no mother and my father existed mainly as my boss. I looked down into my coffee and began spinning my mug around in circles.

"I'm sorry. Sore subject?"

I looked up at him, surprised he seemed to have read my thoughts.

"You're response wasn't very…enthusiastic. You looked sad actually."

Hmmm… he was gorgeous and perceptive; how intriguing.

"It can be a bit trying, but the job isn't really the problem," I said, feeling strangely comfortable talking to him.

"It never is," he said, looking down.

"What do you mean?"

"I just mean when people are stressed out at a job or anything they do in life, it isn't the situation that's bothering them. It's usually that they're judging themselves about something."

"Are you a psychiatrist?"

He chuckled and his cheeks turned pink.

"No, I work night security at the Metropolitan Museum of Art."

"I've seen you before…sitting at the bus stop across the street from my building." The second I said it I regretted it. His back stiffened and he took a sip from his coffee.

"If you work nights, when do you sleep? You must be tired."

"I sleep before work."

I'd obviously touched a nerve. Okay, note to self: too soon to talk about specifics.

Just then I heard the bell ring as the door to the diner opened. I turned around and there was Sam, dripping wet but still smiling. He walked over to the booth.

"Excuse me Ms. Callahan, but the car is all ready to go whenever you are."

"Thanks Sam. I'll be right out."

Sam nodded and left.

"Well, it was really nice meeting you Jo…I mean Lucas. I hope to see you again sometime."

"Now you know where to come whenever you want good pancakes," he said, smiling.

I turned around at the door. He was watching me and I put a hand up in a goodbye wave. He smiled as he returned the gesture.

ॐ◌ल

The next day when I got to work I walked passed reception hearing 'Walk Like an Egyptian.' It put a skip in my step as I sauntered down the quiet hallway and into my office. I dropped my briefcase on the floor and sat down behind my desk, feeling different, like something was changing maybe? Karen came in, already in full working mode.

"Hey, a few messages," she said as she laid three pink pieces of paper on my desk.

"Already? I just got here for crying out loud. Let me guess…Mr. Donovan?" I rolled my eyes.

"He's anxious for you to meet a new witness. I told him all three times he called that you weren't in yet but that you would call him as soon as you could."

"Thank you Karen," I said. I looked out the window as I took a big swallow of my mocha. "Did you have a good night?" I wasn't ready to begin another day of work; the kind that had the same beginning, middle and end. I wanted to hear about what regular people did.

"Yeah, it was fine, I guess. Jim and I saw a movie and that's about it really. How about you?" I could hear the confusion in her voice. Karen and I never talked about personal things. She started shuffling through papers behind me.

"Oh, I did the usual; nothing." Nothing except meet a gorgeous man.

As I took another sip of coffee I looked over at Lucas sitting across the street on his bench. Lucas. He had a name now and it sounded good echoing through my head. He was looking straight ahead and I tried to figure out where his gaze was focused. I leaned forward a bit but I couldn't see anything all that interesting; just people coming and going from the court house.

"Did you ever see that guy who sits on that bench over there all day?" I asked Karen.

"Yeah, I've seen him, why?"

"I just wonder what he's doing there."

"Maybe he's homeless."

"He can't be homeless, he's too well dressed." And too good looking. "I don't know. I guess it doesn't matter." I spun back around to my desk and picked up my messages. I needed to start work or I would day dream about Lucas all morning long. "I'd better call Mr. Donovan back. I'll need a spot for the end of the week sometime in case I need to have this new witness come in. What does my schedule look like?"

"Thursday afternoon or Friday morning are your only free times."

"Okay, if need be I'll send him to you to set up a time." I picked up the phone and started dialing. As much as I wanted to, I couldn't put off my day any longer.

൙

After reassuring Mr. Donovan that the case of check fraud against him was going fine and his need for witnesses was unnecessary, I couldn't focus on work at all. I couldn't stop thinking about Lucas and decided I needed to know more about him. Where did he live? Was he married? Did he have kids? I had to call Lamb.

"Hello Jen, how the hell are ya?"

"Hey Lamb, I'm good. Did I catch you at a bad time?"

"No, no, I'm just sittin' here havin' my coffee." I pictured him sitting in his cargo shorts and tacky Hawaiian shirt, feet in slippers propped up on the coffee table. "How's your dad?"

"Oh he's the same," I said, rolling my eyes. "Hey, I was hoping I could get some help on this…case I'm working on."

"Okay, sure, what can I do for ya?"

"Well, I only have a couple of basic things right now but I figured with your connections that should be enough."

"Basic is usually enough. Let's hear what 'cha got."

"I have a first name, Lucas, and his occupation is night security at the Metropolitan Museum of Art." I began twirling my hair as a pang of guilt clutched my stomach.

"And what is it you would like to know about this fella; criminal background, financial status?"

"For starters just a full name and an address will be enough." I didn't want to pry into Lucas's life too much. I just wanted to get a feel for who he was.

"Okay, if you're sure that's all, I can probably have that for ya by lunch time."

"Thanks Lamb, I appreciate it."

"Okay honey, I'll give you a shout later on."

I hung up the phone and turned to look out the window. There was Lucas, sitting on his bench just as he always did, unaware that I was invading his privacy. I felt a bit ashamed that I was being sneaky but I needed to know. Meeting Lucas had re-ignited a fire in me that had gone out so long ago I had almost forgotten what it felt like. The monotony of my daily life had been weighing heavily on me lately; coming and going to work, client meetings, even court didn't give me the thrill it used to any more. It was exhilarating wondering about Lucas's story and I liked that feeling, I missed that feeling. I wasn't doing any harm by finding out his full name. That was harmless enough.

❧

I was distracted all morning, waiting for Lamb to call. Finally the phone rang just before I was leaving for lunch.

"So I found out what you wanted. His full name is Lucas Benjamin which I thought sounded familiar. He has a Queens' address and sure enough, I know this fella."

I began twirling my hair as Lamb spoke. Maybe I didn't want to hear the rest of the information.

"He was an NYPD detective working undercover for a big drug business." I looked at Lucas. I could see that about him; that he used to be a detective. No wonder he had been good at reading me the other night. "Somehow his cover was blown and a few days later his parents were found murdered. It isn't a pretty story Jen. All of this comes from hunches and speculation, but it seems pretty clear that whoever runs the business sent Lucas a message. They broke into his parents' house, beat them to a pulp, all before dousing the place with gas and setting it on fire. They were still alive, tied up left to die. Lucas ran into the building, tried to save them, but it was too late."

I had my hand over my mouth. I couldn't have made up a more horrific story.

"My buddy told me Lucas had a breakdown and went into the looney bin. When he got out he didn't remember a thing about his parents or the fire; none of it. He couldn't go back to the police department so that's why he's working security."

I sat up straight. "Wait a minute. So you're telling me he has amnesia?" I couldn't believe how bizarre all of it sounded.

"It's a kind of post-traumatic stress amnesia. The person is so traumatized by an event that they block it out of their mind. The severity of the effect depends on the person and how much they can remember."

As I sat thinking about all that Lamb had just told me, it dawned on me; none of it explained why he sat on that bench all day.

"Is this Lucas Benjamin a witness of yours or something?" Lamb asked, interrupting my thoughts. "Do you have a new case you're working on?"

I didn't know what to tell him so I opted for nothing. "Thanks for the info, Lamb. I have to go. I'll be in touch."

I hung up before he had a chance to argue with me. I looked at the picture of my mother on my desk and traced the outline of her face. I remembered the day I was told she had died as though it was yesterday. My father was in the living room standing with his arms folded, staring out the window. He looked distraught, standing perfectly still. My mother's sister, my Aunt Gracie, enveloped me into a strong embrace, sobbing into my small neck. I was so confused and didn't understand what was going on. Why was everybody acting so weird? Through heaves of breath she finally told me that my mother had been in a car accident and had died. I must have gone into shock as her words seeped into my brain. I looked to my father, hoping for clarity and reassurance. He ignored me. He bowed his head and I remember him looking ashamed as he walked out of the room. The fact that Lucas couldn't remember the terrible night his parents had died seemed like a blessing to me.

త్తిపోల

The next morning at my usual stop for coffee I got an extra cup. When Sam dropped me off in front of my building I waited for the car to pull away and then I crossed the street. Lucas looked up just as I got to his bench. He stood up to greet me. I couldn't help noticing he looked incredibly handsome in jeans and a polo shirt that was unbuttoned at the collar, exposing dark chest hair.

"Good morning," I said with a big smile. I held the second cup of coffee out to him. "Cream no sugar, right?"

"Good morning, yes, thank you." I watched the muscles flex on his forearm as he took the cup from me. Gorgeous, perceptive, and strong too. I was fanning myself internally.

"Can I join you for a moment?" I asked.

He raised his eyebrows and gestured towards the bench for me to sit down.

"I'm sorry if I'm intruding. I just wanted to say hello and ask if you wanted to have pancakes with me sometime." Please ask me out, please ask me out!

A car blew its horn as it went by us and I jumped.

I looked at him; he was trying not to laugh. He took a sip of his coffee as a distraction but it didn't work; I could still see the grin he was trying to hide as he looked at me over the top of his cup. He looked different to me now that I knew about his history. I suddenly felt ashamed for knowing those things.

"I'm sorry; I don't mean to laugh at you. I don't get company very often so you'll have to be patient with me."

I couldn't help but laugh a little too. He was glad I was there. Man, that felt good to hear.

"It's fine. I have to get to work, but think about my offer. I work just across the street." I opened my briefcase and began digging through it. I held out a business card. "All of my contact information is on here."

He took the card and placed it in his back pocket without even looking at it.

"Okay then," I said, getting up.

He stood up too.

"Thanks again for the coffee."

I could feel the heat between us and I flushed. This was out of character for me. I had been alone for so long and had built a wall so high that I didn't think anyone would ever be able to climb to the top. I was in my ivory tower. Could it be I was finally going to be saved? "You're welcome. Good bye Lucas."

"Good bye Jennifer."

We stood with our eyes locked for a moment and all I could think about was kissing him. I wanted to reach out and touch the stubble on his cheek and run my fingers through the curls at his neck. I slowly turned and crossed the street. Before I went inside, I looked back. He was sitting looking at my business card. I smiled, mentally jumping up and punching the air.

Chapter Three

Three long days passed without any word from Lucas. I tried my best to go about my daily business without thinking about him but it was impossible with him sitting across the street from my office all day. In fact, it was incredibly distracting. I would find myself watching him out of my window, remembering what a gentleman he was and how confident he had been when he asked me to join him in the diner. He'd seemed comfortable with me at the bus stop, playful even. I made up opportunities in my head I could create between us in which we could meet again. We would get to know each other and become friends, then, when he was comfortable with me maybe he would tell me why he sat out there all day. Truthfully I didn't really care about that anymore. I was more curious about what those amazing lips would feel like kissing my neck. I wonder if he's a good kisser. It had been so long since I had been with a man, my libido was running on overdrive.

Inevitably someone would walk into my office and catch me. I would compose myself and wonder if my flushed cheeks were noticeable. Daydreaming about a drop dead gorgeous man can do that to a woman and work had been the furthest thing from my mind.

My best friend Roxanne had been bugging me about going to the gym for a class. She'd always had such a good grasp on life and her mind was always so focused. She'd obviously been doing something right. I'd missed confiding in her about my life, but I gave that up months ago. How could I expect her to keep giving me advice about changing things when I was unwilling to do anything different? I could use a sounding board right about now, that was for sure.

I picked up the phone and called Karen. I told her not to schedule anything for Friday afternoon and that I would be leaving after lunch.

❧

At Clay, a prestigious health club on West 14th Street, I met up with Roxanne in the locker room. She and I had been friends since college where we had hit it off immediately. She could read me like I was an open book, which pissed me off, but I appreciated it. I really only confided in her when it came to my personal life. She worked as a personal trainer. She was beautiful too; tall and thin with a strong, muscular body. She was the epitome of health; the exact opposite to me.

"I haven't heard from you in almost two weeks, Jen. What's going on with you? Did you meet someone?"

I laughed out loud as I tugged on my spandex tank top. Exercise clothes never looked as good on me as they did on Roxanne. Why did they have to put the goddamn mirror right where we could all see ourselves dressing?

"No I didn't meet anyone, come on. I've just been busy…working on a new case." I wondered if she would buy that answer. I remembered too late that Roxanne had a very good way of reading me. Shit.

She stood over me with her hands on her hips. "Tell me what's going on. It must be something that's really bothering you if you're here."

"I'm working on something new," I said, avoiding her gaze.

"Okay, what is it that you're working on?"

I sat on the bench in front of the lockers and tied my running shoes while I tried to figure out how to tell her about Lucas. When I was done making bows I leaned on my knees and started at the beginning. I explained it as if all I cared about was trying to figure out why Lucas sat on the bench. I wasn't ready to tell her how attracted to him I had become.

"Well, why does he sit there all day?"

"That's the million dollar question."

I stood up. I felt bad knowing what I did about Lucas and I was beginning to feel worse for telling someone else about it.

"Let's get started on a workout, okay? I didn't come here to talk about this."

She took my arm lightly. "When you're ready to talk, I'm here, okay?"

"I know. Thank you."

We walked out of the locker room in silence. I wasn't sure myself how I felt anymore. Meeting Lucas had sparked something new in me and I didn't know how to explain it just yet. When we got upstairs Roxanne turned all business on me again, taking me from machine to machine. She didn't bring up Lucas again.

After my workout, I left Roxanne so she could start a late session with a client. I decided to sit in the sauna for a while. I had to admit that the workout had felt really good, but I was sure I'd regret it the next day. I sat back and leaned my head against the wall and closed my eyes. I wasn't sure why, but I'd really been missing my mom over the past few weeks. She had been such a patient person, sophisticated and refined. She had been sixteen years younger than my father when they married, got pregnant with me right away, which I don't think my father expected. He was a business man not a family man, or so it seemed to me anyway. Maybe he would have rather have had a son. My mother had loved me unconditionally though and took care of everything I needed until the day she died. I remember her looking like a princess every time she and my father went to some banquet or fundraiser, but she was never afraid to get dirty while playing with me.

I decided I had had enough of the sauna when the heat, and my memories, became too unbearable. After a cool shower and getting dressed, I was feeling pretty exhausted. I got out my phone to call Sam to meet me out front and saw there was a new voice mail message. I checked the number and didn't recognize it. I really hoped Karen hadn't given Mr. Donovan my cell number!

I called Sam as I stepped out of the locker room and walked past the indoor basketball courts. After disconnecting from him I called my voice mail.

"Hello Jennifer...ah...this is Lucas. I'm going for pancakes and thought maybe you would want to join me. So...if you're free, I'll see you there."

I was so distracted I almost ran into the smoothie bar in the lobby. Excitement coursed through me, softening every bone in my body. A schoolgirl grin filled my face as I juggled my phone in my shaking hands.

I checked my watch; it was just after five o'clock. I rushed through the lobby to the front doors. Looked like I was having pancakes for dinner tonight.

For the longest time I'd spent my days in exactly the same way; waking up too early, going to work, going home. But since getting to know this... stranger...he was all I could think about. It had been like reading a good book that you just didn't want to put down. I couldn't wait to see what was going to happen the next time I was with him. Would he tell me something more about himself? Would we become friends? I had no idea, but I couldn't wait to find out.

Sam was waiting for me at the curb.

"Hey Sam. I'd like you to take me to the 5th Street Diner instead of home, please."

Our eyes met in the rear view mirror and I read the look of confusion he was sending me. I ignored him and pulled a compact out of my purse to give myself a quick once over. I wasn't feeling as confident as I would have had I had the time to prepare for meeting someone for dinner, but I would just have to do. I applied a little pink lip gloss and left it at that.

After what seemed like an eternity, the car pulled over in front of the diner.

"Here we are," Sam said. He looked at me. "Do you want me to wait for you?"

"Absolutely not, Sam, you go home and I'll see you tomorrow. I'll just catch a cab."

"Are you sure about this, Jen?"

I knew Sam was serious. When he called me by my first name it meant he was off the clock and was my friend, not my employee.

"What do you mean?"

"You've been....different lately. I'm glad to see you finally doing some new things for a change but I just want to make sure you're doing them for the right reasons."

I knew what he meant. He knew all the old stories about me from when I was back in college. I had been behaving like such a robot lately and if anyone was going to notice a change in me it was going to be Sam. I felt my heart pull at the fact that he cared.

"Thanks, Sam," I said, putting my hand on his arm. "I appreciate your concern, but I'm really not doing anything other than making a friend."

I opened the door and stood on the curb, leaning in before closing the door. "Have a good night."

As I walked into the diner I heard the familiar ring of the bell as I pushed open the door. I saw Lucas right away, sitting in the same booth. He looked up and his face softened into a smile. I heard Stevie Wonder singing about superstition as I walked towards him, our eyes never leaving each other. He stood up. He was wearing a t-shirt, gym shorts and running shoes, and his hair looked damp from sweat. My face flushed as my heart started racing.

"Hi," he said. "I wasn't sure if you would get my message or not."

"I got it not too long ago actually. I was just leaving the gym so it was perfect timing."

"I just got here myself. I was out for a run."

W both sat down and he handed me a menu. I took it with a smile.

"So what's good here besides the pancakes?" I asked as I skimmed the few items.

"I couldn't tell ya, the pancakes are all I've ever gotten."

An image of what my figure would look like if I ate pancakes four times a week popped into my head. I doubted sweat pants would be proper court attire.

Gerry came and took our drinks order. Only a minute went by before she returned with two cups of coffee. Lucas handed me the cream with a big grin on his face, obviously pleased with himself for remembering.

"Thank you," I said. "You're such a gentleman."

I poured some cream into my mug and reached for some sugar as well. When I looked back at Lucas he had a blank expression on his face; almost as though he was in a trance. I looked at him for a moment until finally I reached my hand across the table and touched his arm.

"Lucas? Are you alright?"

He blinked a couple of times. He looked confused and sad.

"Is everything alright?" I asked again.

His body stiffened and he pulled his arm away from my hand. He gathered his keys from the table and stood up.

"I'm sorry…I have to leave."

I stood up but he was gone and out the door before I had a chance to do or say anything. I slumped back down into the booth and tried to figure out what had just happened. What had I said? Had I done something to offend him?

Gerry came over. I looked up at her blankly, unable to find any words.

"Don't hold it against him honey. Lucas has been through…a lot."

"You mean his parents." I looked down at the table.

"Oh, I wasn't…I didn't know you knew." She paused.

I stood up to leave, and then turned to Gerry.

"You don't know where he lives, do you?"

She paused. "He lives a couple of blocks up in a building on the corner. It has a red awning over the front door."

My instincts were telling me she was reluctant to tell me much. "Thanks." Impulsively, I embraced her tightly, grateful for her help. I turned quickly and dashed to the door.

"He's been through enough," she called after me.

I waved a hand in the air without turning around.

As I walked down the sidewalk in the direction Gerry had pointed, my heart was racing and my mind was flooded with uncertainty. Would he want me there? Was he angry with me? I didn't know what to think but my gut was telling me to go to him. Or was it my heart?

I reached the end of the second block and started to wonder if I was going in the wrong direction. It was dark but the street lamps were blazing orange rays. I walked onto the third block, saw a red awning, but still wasn't sure if it was right or not. I scanned the line of buzzers. At the end I saw 'L.B.' That had to stand for Lucas Benjamin.

I pushed the buzzer and waited. No response. I pushed it again. Maybe he'd left for work already. Maybe he hadn't even come back here.

"Yes?"

Oh thank God, he was there. "Lucas?"

"Yes, can I help you?"

"It's Jennifer…can we talk?"

There was silence.

The buzzer went off at the door and I heard a click. I pulled the door open and immediately noticed the lobby smelled musty and dirty. I scanned the mail boxes and found his apartment number was 4C. The old, rickety elevator was out of order, not that I was planning to use it anyway. That's all I needed - to be stuck in the elevator. After skipping stairs to the fourth floor, I found his door without any trouble, but had to stop for a moment to catch my breath. I would have thought that with the workout, along with my adrenaline, I would have been in better shape. After composing myself, I knocked lightly on the door.

When Lucas answered, I wasn't sure what to say. My heart was pounding in my ears and my stomach was full of butterflies. His hair was wet and he was wearing khaki pants and a white dress shirt rolled up at the sleeves, looking fresh and smelling clean from a shower. He looked amazing and for a moment I was distracted by the urge to kiss him.

He stepped aside. "Come in."

The place was small with a living room and kitchen side by side. It was simply decorated and furnished with a black sofa and a brown leather chair. There were no pictures on the walls. A small hallway beyond the living room led to the back of the apartment, probably to the bathroom and bedroom. Although it was small, it was clean and organized; much more so than what I had expected from the lobby.

"Did you follow me?"

I turned to face him. "No...I asked the waitress. I was worried...I wanted to make sure you were alright." I began nervously wringing my hands. "You left so abruptly." My thoughts were swimming, along with my emotions.

He sat on the sofa, leaning his arms on his knees. I slowly followed him, trying to gauge his behavior, hoping to anticipate what he would say or do. I sat down in the chair.

"I'm sorry," he said, looking into his folded hands.

My heart ached, thinking he had no reason to apologize to me. I was the one who should be apologizing! "Did I do something to upset you?"

He pushed his eyebrows together and looked at me as though he was about to speak. Then he looked back down.

"I'm not really sure what happened," he said softly.

My confusion deepened but I didn't reply. What I really wanted to do was to sit next to him and tell him it was okay and that he could trust me. Instead, I just sat there like a statue. I watched the muscles in his forearms flex as he began knotting his fingers. He seemed to be in such pain.

"I've been having these...flashes I guess you could call it. Every now and then I'll see images that I don't understand but they make me feel like shit."

I couldn't fight the urge any more. I went over to the sofa and sat next to him. I put my hand on his arm and he watched as I gently squeezed it.

"Do you want to talk about it?" I asked.

He looked up at me, confused.

"I don't know...when you said I was a gentleman it reminded me of my mom." He shrugged a shoulder. "When I saw you looking at me I felt like a freak or something, so I just left. Not the best way for me to behave and I'm sorry for that."

He sat back and sighed heavily. The feel of his skin lingered on my hand. His face was etched with anguish as he rubbed the back of his neck. I scolded myself for pushing him to talk about things that made him sad. I waited patiently as he found his words.

"It's been...about a year ago now since I was released from a mental hospital. It's funny how fast the time has gone by. I was told that I was in a bad accident and I had lost my memory. I knew that was a bunch of shit because I knew my name, what year it was and that I was a detective working undercover. I just didn't remember how I got there or what had happened. I had a meeting with a shrink and he told me my parents had died and that I had been seriously injured while trying to save them. It didn't make any sense to me and it pissed me off that I couldn't remember any of it. Apparently that's normal." He made quote marks in the air. "And eventually I would remember. My sergeant told me my cover had been blown and since the undercover case I was working was compromised he wanted me in witness protection right away. I refused; told him I needed to figure things out here, not in some strange town."

I sat watching him, trying to read his face, maybe the tone of his voice. But his words were flat and disconnected, unemotional.

"After that we argued for a long time. Sarge kept insisting my life was in danger and it wasn't safe for me in the city. But there was no way I could leave. It was my fault my parents died. I took off, hopped on a bus and went to my mom's house. When I got off the bus, there was just a bunch of rubble and ash where the house used to be. I walked around and kicked through the debris, hoping something would trigger my memory. I saw burned up pictures and other things from the house. It just made me so mad." He took a deep breath and looked down at the floor. "So I got back on the bus. When it stopped on Madison I got off across from the court house building. I had been having the same dream since I woke up in the hospital, which still wakes me up to this day. I see two men coming out of the court house walking together, celebrating like something really good had just happened. I recognize them in my dream, but I can't remember who they are; I feel like I know them from somewhere. They look over at me and start to laugh, and then I wake up. The dream seems so real and I can never figure out what it means."

He sighed heavily and continued.

"I had no family, no job and just a couple bucks in the bank. The apartment I was living in had been rented out because I'd been in the hospital for a long time. Eventually I got hungry after sitting at the bus stop for a while so I walked to the diner I met you in. The waitress, Gerry, was pretty cool. She must have noticed I was kind of lost by the way I was acting. We got to talking and she told me about an empty place in her building which is this castle you see here." He extended his hands.

"After a couple weeks of feeling sorry for myself I found a job and got back in touch with a couple of guys from the station. Sitting on the bench at the court house helps for some reason. Watching people has become what I do now. Some days I hope I'll see the men from my dream and maybe I'll remember something."

He looked over at me. I was shocked that he had just confessed all of that to me but at the same time warmed by the fact that he trusted me enough to do so. I just wished I had waited for him to tell me himself instead of going behind his back.

"I don't know why I just told you all that but you came here after me so I figured I owed you an explanation. Not really first date conversation I guess."

First date? Was that what this was?

He stood up and went to the fridge. He got himself out a bottle of water and held another one out to me.

"No thanks, I'm fine."

He opened his water and took a long drink.

"I used to talk to a shrink after I got out of the hospital. That was all bullshit though because it didn't do a thing to help me remember anything. It seems like everybody thinks I'm gonna lose my mind or something." He laughed a little. "Oh wait, I forgot, I already have." He took another long drink from his water.

"I'm sorry that happened to you," I said in a quiet voice. "I know what it's like losing a parent. My mom died in a car accident when I was seven. I work with my father but we're more like colleagues really. I miss my mom a lot and wonder sometimes what I'd be doing if she were still alive right now."

"You don't like being a lawyer?"

"Yeah, I do I guess," I said with a shrug. "It's what my father raised me to do but my mom always encouraged me to do what I wanted. When she wasn't around anymore it was easier just to do what my father told me. After school I went to college. I was a bit wild, graduating by the skin of my teeth. I got into trouble all the time. After law school I passed the bar, barely. My father offered me a job but it didn't come without a warning: the first time I messed up I would be out of a job, at his firm anyway." I rolled my eyes and felt my face flush with anger as I spoke. "I threw myself into work in the first few years, saying no to no one, especially my father. I loved everything about it at first; the power, the confidence and winning. But now…now I'm not really even sure what I want anymore."

It dawned on me that I was feeling sorry for myself and talking about stuff that didn't even compare to what Lucas had gone through.

"I must not be the only one in the world who needs to figure something out, huh?" he said with a grin.

I looked at him and saw a different man. He was confident and smart. Even after all he had been through, he still had a strong attitude and a sense of humor.

"So what are you going to do?"

"What do you mean?" he asked. "Do about what?"

"About what happened; I assume you still want to know, right?"

He drank the rest of the water from the bottle and slowly screwed the cap back on as he considered my question. He put the bottle down and sat back down on the couch, knotting his hands behind his head.

"I don't know. My parents are dead and a bunch of assholes killed them. I would like nothing more than to get the guy responsible. The only problem with that is I can't prove it - I don't remember."

"Yeah, I guess so. Do you think you'll ever be a police officer again?"

"If it were up to me I'd be doing that right now. Apparently I didn't pass the exam the department shrink gave me so I don't make the cut anymore."

"It sounds to me like you need a distraction," I said cheerfully. "Your butt is gonna get flat sitting on that bench all the time." I nudged him playfully.

He laughed. "And what do you suggest I do instead?"

"Maybe you could find a day job. It's better than looking for mystery men on the court house steps all day, right?"

"And would you help me occupy my nights?"

Holy shit, he was flirting with me! I blushed. I ran my hands up and down my thighs as my imagination ran wild, thinking of nights spent with Lucas. Sounded good to me!

He nudged me back. "Don't be so uptight, Jen. I was joking, so you can relax."

I scowled internally, disappointed. Lucas was no longer that weak, pathetic man I saw outside my window. Hell, I wanted to spend the night with him.

"Look, I hate to break this little party up but if I'm going to make it to work tonight I'm going to need to finish getting ready."

"Oh…sure…" I stood up and looked around, stalling. I didn't want to leave. "Well then, I guess I'll see you around." I'll see you around? Don't leave it like that you idiot! I walked towards the door.

"Since we never got to eat tonight how 'bout I make it up to you; I'd love to take you to dinner."

Yes! He was asking me out! "I would really like that," I said.

"I'll give you a call then. Think about where you might want to go 'cos I'm getting pretty sick of pancakes."

"Okay, great...I'll talk to you soon then." I turned to open the door but stopped myself and turned back to face him. "Thank you for trusting me with everything you told me tonight."

"I haven't trusted someone in a long time, so thank you."

When I got outside the air was chilly. I hugged myself but wasn't convinced the goosebumps were just from the cold. I was pretty sure it was because I was absolutely giddy. It took forever to hail a cab. I felt tired...tired for the first time in such a long time.

I lay in bed, wondering what Lucas was doing. I imagined him walking confidently through the empty halls of the museum. I wondered if he was thinking of me too. I hugged my pillow tight, wishing it was him.

Chapter Four

I fell asleep easily and the next thing I knew it was 9:43 the next morning. I was late!

How could I not have heard the alarm? I felt frazzled, dashing out of bed, not really knowing where to begin my morning routine. Should I bother with a shower? Should I make coffee? I hadn't ever been late to work. I found my phone and saw two messages. Shit! I called Karen right away. "Your father was looking for you. He seemed upset when he couldn't reach you by phone." I thanked her and hung up. Oh great, my father was in the office. Of all the days to oversleep!

I took a quick shower and took a cab to work. Where was Sam? Why hadn't he rung the buzzer? That would have woken me up. I couldn't blame him; it was my fault I was about to get it when I got to work. As I got out of the cab I glanced over and saw that Lucas wasn't sitting on the bench and my heart sank.

By the time I got out of the elevator it was 10:30. I walked quickly, trying to look as though I was coming from a stressful meeting and hadn't just overslept. I dashed straight to my office, avoiding Rosemarie, closed the door behind me and slumped into my chair. I felt like I could breathe now. I spun around and looked at the empty bench outside. Where was he?

I heard my office door open and turned around to see my father, his shoulders squared and his arms folded. The expression on his face was as grey as his pinstriped suit.

"Oh, good morning Daddy," I said, pushing papers around, trying to look busy.

"I can almost say good afternoon," he said.

Oh great, he's gonna scold me now? It isn't even that late, he's so dramatic. "Yes, well I had an early meeting this morning. It was last minute and I didn't think it would take as long as it did." I didn't look at him. I didn't want him to read my eyes. He always knew when I was lying.

"If that's true Jennifer, next time call Karen and let her know please.

I would prefer all meetings with clients be here in the office. I want to keep things as professional as possible. Is that too much to ask?"

"Of course not, I apologize."

I could feel my entire body start to shake. I couldn't tell if it was because I was nervous or angry. Probably both, but either way I didn't want my father to see it. I couldn't stand the thought of him seeing me as weak. I felt like getting up and slapping him, demanding to know why he had to treat me like a child. Why was he making such a big deal out of this anyway?

"I tried to call you as well. I don't like the idea of you being unreachable. Unless it wasn't a client you were with?"

"I had my phone off. Look, I said I was sorry. It won't happen again." I was beginning to resent his accusing tone. I worked harder than anyone in this place.

"Yes, well I appreciate that. I'll let you get back to work then."

He closed the door and I couldn't hold my emotions back anymore. I began sobbing, as quietly as I could so no one would hear, with my hands over my face. I picked up a pencil and threw it across the room. It was the only thing I could find that wouldn't bring attention to my office. It bounced off a bookcase, rolling to a stop on the floor. I wished it could have been a coffee mug. I glanced at the picture of my mother and wished she were there right now to save me from my father's temper like she used to do. She had never been afraid to hug me and had never hesitated to tell me things would be okay. A memory of her and me dancing in the backyard took over. I was in one of her dresses that was way too big for me and she was wearing a long sundress. She spun me around and around until we were both dizzy, laughing in a heap in the grass.

This wasn't what I wanted anymore. Working here wasn't what I should be doing with my time; my life. The conversation with Lucas last night had made me see that. After all he had been through, he was still moving on with his life. But what else was there for me? All I'd ever known was how to be a lawyer. My father had molded me into exactly what he wanted and now I knew nothing else. But he had also taught me how to be a fighter.

I had so many things in my life that I took for granted. My father knew exactly what to say to make me doubt myself - enough that I would just give in and say forget it; I'll be sorry if I don't listen to him. I wished

I could crumple up this chapter of my life and throw it out. I could start over; rewrite it and make my own decisions and mistakes.

I opened up the calendar on my computer and checked the next month. I had two weeks' worth of appointments and court scheduled so far and nothing after that. I blocked the last week of the month off and decided it was time I took a vacation. My father had kept the beach house in North Carolina after my mother had died; I'd go there for a week.

&~&

The next few days I was busy in court and I didn't hear from Lucas. A couple of times I considered going to his apartment to surprise him with take-out. But I talked myself out of it, convincing myself I had no business to burst in on him whenever I wanted. I grew more anxious as every boring day went by, wondering when, or if, he was going to call. I felt like a teenager, checking my phone constantly.

Saturday morning I woke up, again, at 4:30. After I'd overslept and been late to work, my sub-conscience was back to getting me up early. I made coffee and worked in the living room on notes for court the following Monday. I sat on the sofa with my computer on my lap as the morning turned into afternoon without me even noticing. My cell phone rang and I barely noticed that either. With a pencil in my mouth and my eyes on my computer screen I answered.

"Hello," I said without looking to see who it was.

"Jennifer?"

I let the pencil drop from my mouth and sat up. "Yes?" My heart beat picked up.

"Wow, it didn't even sound like you. I thought I had the wrong number for a second there." There was a long pause. "This is Lucas. Did I catch you at a bad time?"

I put my computer on the coffee table and got up so I could pace around. All of a sudden I was giddy and flustered

"No, I'm just sitting here working on a case for next week."

"If you're busy we can talk another time."

"No! I mean, I'm not doing anything critical. How have you been?"

He was laughing a little. "I'm good. I've actually been busy looking for a day job. I thought about what you said the other night and figured it wasn't such a bad idea. What the hell, right?"

"That's great! How's the search going?""

"Pretty good. I got in touch with my old partner. We got to talking and he put me onto a firm that needed security. I had an interview at some government building downtown, nothing fancy. My buddy Mac put in a good word for me. We'll see I guess."

"That's really great. I can't believe how fast that happened! I mean, you just decided you wanted to do something different and you did it."

I thought about my own situation and how I wanted to get out from under my father's shadow. Just the thought scared the hell out of me.

"I don't have the job so don't congratulate me just yet. What've you been up to all week? Missed me?"

He had that flirty tone to his voice again. I felt my face get warm and hated that I didn't know if he was being serious or not. If I were honest I would say yes, I thought about you every day and was disappointed every time I didn't see you on that stupid bench.

"I've just been working. I'm going to be heading to the beach for a vacation in a couple of weeks so I'm trying to finish everything up and tidy last minute details."

"Ah, the beach; great place to fish."

"I don't plan on doing anything while I'm there. Maybe I'll find a book to read or something."

"So you're going alone then?"

Not unless you want to come with me. "Yep."

"Well, I'm hoping you don't feel like being alone tonight. I was calling to see if you wanted to do dinner. But if you're busy working we can do it some other time."

"I would love to have dinner."

"Okay, good. You like Italian? Cos I know this great place downtown."

"Yeah, that sounds good. I can meet you there."

❧❧

Lucas was waiting for me on the sidewalk. He looked like a model straight out of GQ. He was wearing black dress pants and a light blue short-sleeved golf shirt. His shoulders were broad and he had a day or two of stubble on his face. The muscles flexed on his arms as he took his hands out of his pants pockets and came to greet me.

"You look beautiful," he said. And without skipping a beat he leaned in and kissed my cheek. I could feel the stubble on his chin. I closed my eyes, enjoying his touch.

I thought back to the nervous primping I had done all afternoon in anticipation of seeing him again. I must have tried on ten outfits before finally deciding on a black pencil skirt and a sleeveless white top. I felt slightly underdressed compared to him but the butterflies in my stomach from his kiss distracted me enough that I didn't care anymore what I was wearing.

"Thank you. You don't look so bad yourself."

"Well, let's have some dinner, shall we?"

I felt awkward for the first few minutes. I scolded myself - I was a confident attorney. Dinner should have been a walk in the park compared to court. But Lucas wasn't just anyone to me anymore. The more I thought about it, the more I realized how much I liked him. I'd take court any day.

We made small talk until our meals came. I was becoming more relaxed, enjoying the break in the monotony of my usual weekends. He asked about my mother and I found I was comfortable talking about her, telling him things I hadn't thought about in a long time, like how I envied her creativity and how good she was with her hands. I had never been creative but always gave it a try anyway. My painting of a scene at the beach was pathetic in comparison to my mother's, but it ended up on the fridge, which made me proud. I told him about the beach house and the summers we used to spend there. When he asked about my father I became rigid, and Lucas changed the subject.

When we had finished with dinner, we were asked if we wanted dessert.

"I'm not sure," I said, looking to Lucas.

"Why don't we get something and share it?"

"Okay, that'll work," We chose a chocolate lava cake, something we both agreed looked too good to pass up, and continued talking.

The evening was going so well I couldn't have asked for anything more. Lucas and I were having a great conversation, we seemed to have a few things in common, and it felt like we were old friends catching up.

"Well, hello there Jen." Suddenly my easy going mood came to a crashing halt.

I looked up to see Lamb. My stomach jumped into my throat and I began to panic. The last person in the world I had expected to see was George Lambert. I looked around behind him, wondering who he was here with. Please don't let him be here working with Daddy! I didn't see anyone I recognized. I looked wide-eyed at Lucas; he was calmly looking at Lamb, smiling slightly.

"Oh, hey Lamb."

"I haven't heard from you in a while. I assume all is going smooth with that new case?"

I looked over to Lucas again to see him still smiling as if nothing was wrong. And why would there be? He had no idea the 'case' Lamb was referring to was actually him. I could feel heat start to creep up my back as my frustration began to build. I silently cursed Lamb in language a lady shouldn't use.

"Mm, yes, thank you."

"Well, aren't you going to introduce me?" he asked.

Damn you Lamb! "Oh, of course…Lamb, this is Lucas. Lucas, this is George Lambert. He's my father's oldest friend and partner at the firm."

Lucas stood up as Lamb looked at me then back to Lucas. Lamb had that obvious look of 'what the hell are you doing' written all over his face as his eyes met mine again.

"It's nice to meet you," Lucas said, shaking his hand.

"And you as well," Lamb said, clapping Lucas on the shoulder. "I'll let you two get back to your dinner. I'll speak to you soon, huh Jen?"

"Absolutely."

Lucas and I watched as Lamb walked away. My stomach was cramping, riddled with the guilt of knowing what I did about Lucas and pretending that I didn't. I was angry at Lamb for interrupting the good time I was having. The one night I finally decided to do something and I had to see Lamb. Calm down, Jen.

"What's with the frown?" Lucas asked.

I looked up at him. "I'm sorry, what?"

"You look mad. What's wrong?"

"Oh nothing."

Our dessert came to the table just then. I had no desire to eat it anymore since my stomach was in knots.

"This looks good, doesn't it?"

"I'm feeling full actually. I don't think I can eat another bite."

"What's going on Jen? It's like a switch went off and you're different now."

There was that cop in him again.

"If you're this unhappy after seeing someone from work, you must really hate it there."

I looked at him, surprised that it was so obvious. "It's not that. Well… maybe a little…I don't know." I rubbed my forehead.

"There are firms all over the city that would probably love to have you on their team."

"Thanks, that's nice of you to say. Especially since you have no idea if I'm even good at what I do." I smiled.

"I can tell you're good at what you do. You're confident and articulate. I'm sure you're a shark in the courtroom." He had probably been in the courtroom a few times himself. His compliments were sweet but at that moment I felt undeserving of them.

He took a bite of the chocolate cake. I watched him overplay his reaction with a dramatic look of pleasure on his face; eyes closed and chewing slowly. He had a drip of fudge on the corner of his mouth and I watched as his tongue carefully licked it off. I wanted to crawl across the table and eat him up.

"Mmm, this is too good for you to pass up."

Oh sure it was. I had to look away. I looked down at the cake. It did look really good as I watched the fudge oozing out of the middle like a thick mud slide.

"Here, try a bite."

He reached over with his fork. I reluctantly leaned in and accepted. I couldn't deny the fact that the cake was good, and also that I was happy for the distraction.

"That is good."

"I told you. Now forget about work and let's enjoy the rest of our date."

Work? Who was thinking about work? I picked up my fork.

After dinner Lucas insisted on sharing a cab with me even though I told him I lived on the opposite side of town. He wanted to make sure I got home safe. Is that all? I wondered if he was hoping I would invite him in when we got to my place. Should I? I had been fighting the urge to attack him ever since dessert.

The cab ride was a short one. We came to a stop at the curb and Lucas got out.

"Thank you for a really great evening. I needed this."

"I'm glad," he said. "I had a good time, we should do it again."

There was an uncomfortable silence for a few moments.

"Well, I should go."

Hint, hint, Jennifer! "Thanks again for a wonderful evening." I smiled

He reached down and took my hand. I looked up as he pulled me gently closer to him. He wrapped his arms around my waist and held me tight. My body was flush up against his and I was staring straight at his lips. They were parted slightly and I felt his hands move up my back. He put a hand to the back of my neck and leaned toward me, kissing me slowly at first. He picked up speed as he felt me reciprocate and, before I knew it, my hands were tangling in his hair, which felt exactly how I imagined; soft and thick. He stopped finally, leaving me panting. He moved into my neck and kissed it softly. I felt the prickle of stubble across my skin, making me shiver. Oh my God that felt good! My knees turned to rubber.

"I'll call you tomorrow."

Shit, he was leaving…snap out of it dummy! "Okay."

My heart was pounding as I watched him get in the cab. He waved as the car pulled away. I walked into my apartment and sat on the sofa. I ran through the evening we had just spent together. It was obvious - I was falling for him.

I woke up to the sound of my alarm going off. 6:45 A.M. I had slept through a whole night again. I let my head fall back into the pillow and smiled, knowing it was because I had been with Lucas the night before. For months I had known something was missing from my life, but I hadn't been able to put my finger on what it was. Now I was pretty sure that what had been missing was the excitement of a new relationship. I got up and turned my alarm off. I had to tell him the truth. If things were progressing with us - and it was clear that they were after that kiss - then I needed to be honest. I just needed to figure out how and when. When I got back from the beach, that's when I'd tell him.

Chapter Five

A week had passed. Everything in my daily routine had changed. When I woke up for the day it was after a rested sleep. I no longer went to work filled with resentment or judgement. The dark circles were fading under my eyes since I had been sleeping better, and my skin was pink and rosy. I couldn't wait to get through my day so I could see Lucas again. We had begun to spend every possible moment together. After work I would usually go right to my place to meet him so we could have dinner together before he went to work. A couple of times we had gone running. I hadn't seen my father in a while but that only added to my happiness. Lucas no longer sat on the bench across from the office. He was spending time in the gym down at the police station and looking for day time job opportunities.

I sighed as Lucas rubbed my feet. I'd finished work early as it was Memorial Day, and Lucas had the day off.

"Mmm….that feels sooooo good."

"I don't know why you ladies insist on wearing shoes with heels so high." He was pushing his thumb deep into the arch of my left foot. It was heavenly.

The devil in me perked up. "I bet if I was wearing nothing but those shoes right now you wouldn't be complaining."

I felt him stop massaging for a moment before starting again. I giggled to myself.

I felt his hand traveling up my leg, massaging as he went. After being on my feet most of the day in court, it felt really good. He inched his way up my thigh and then up under my skirt. I opened one eye at him.

"What do you think you're doing?"

He pulled at the top of my thigh high stocking and began rolling it down, pulling it off over my foot.

"Taking these itchy things off….just trying to make you more comfortable, that's all."

"Uh huh." I knew exactly what he was doing and it was making my groin want to spontaneously combust. He moved over to my other leg, repeating the process, and I reluctantly allowed it to continue.

"Why don't you take your top off and I'll rub your back for a while?"

"Nice try bub," I said, getting up and standing over him with my hands on my hips. "I know what you're trying to do and it's not going to work."

"What?"

"If I let this go any further, I'm going to be completely naked."

"Would that be such a bad thing?" He stood up and wrapped his arms around my waist. He started kissing my neck, something I was sure he knew by now drove me absolutely crazy.

"I thought we were going for a run, remember?" He stopped mid-kiss and pulled back.

"Yeah…right…a run. That's exactly what I wanted to do."

"That's not sarcasm I hear, is it, Detective?"

"Me? Sarcastic? No way. I'm gonna go change. I'll meet you back out here in five minutes, okay?"

"Okay."

I knew he was disappointed. It had been incredibly hard for me to stop him…again. There had been a couple of times when things between us had gotten really heated and intense like that. It took every fiber of my being to resist him and stop, remembering the promise I had made to myself about telling him the truth. He had never pressed me though. He was a perfect gentleman.

I grabbed my duffle bag and went into the bathroom to change into my running clothes. After a long day at work I wasn't particularly thrilled about going running but we needed the distraction. When I came out Lucas was all ready and waiting for me. I loved how he looked in workout clothes, especially when he was wearing shorts. His body was lean and muscular and he was in really good shape.

"You ready?" he asked.

"Yep."

We walked to the corner and began running as we crossed the street. We kept a steady pace and set on a three mile course that Lucas ran frequently. It was such a beautiful day; warmer than the previous weeks had been. The sky was blue and the air had that smell of spring. People were out all over the city riding bikes and taking walks. Kids were playing catch in the street and neighbors sat on stoops chatting.

We were coming up on the last leg of our route and I was feeling really worn out. I was sweating and thirsty. I couldn't wait to get to the part where we stopped and walked our cool down.

"You're slowing down…you okay?" Lucas asked, looking back at me over his shoulder.

"Yeah, I'm fine. Don't worry about me."

"One more block and we can walk. You wanna race?"

Hell no, I didn't wanna race, dammit. But I didn't tell him that. I picked up my pace and yelled "Go!" as I ran past him.

"Hey…"

He caught up to me with ease and taunted me, pretending to let me win and then running ahead again. We finally reached the end of the block and I came to a halt and began to walk, heaving and puffing to catch my breath.

"Don't stop walking or you'll cramp up." I nodded with a wave of my hand, not able to answer. A minute later I was breathing a bit more regularly but my heart was pounding in my ears. I was so hot and thirsty, I felt like I was going to faint. I was so out of shape.

By the time we reached Lucas's block, I was fantasizing about a tall glass of ice water dripping with condensation. I would take the glass and smear it on my cheeks and then take a long drink of the water. Then I would pour the rest of it over my head.

I looked over at Lucas and noticed he had an anguished look on his face. The skin around his eyes was bunched up as he stared at something across the street. I followed his gaze and saw that there was a man leaning against the railing of some stairs that led up to a brownstone. He was wearing black pants and a black short-sleeved polo shirt, dark sunglasses hid his eyes and he had his arms folded.

"Who's that?" I asked.

"I don't know but I don't like him."

I looked back at the man and didn't see anything unusual about him. "Maybe he's waiting for someone."

"Maybe."

When we got up to Lucas's apartment I made a bee-line for the refrigerator for bottled water. I grabbed two and didn't waste any time in opening mine. I took three long pulls and had to stop to catch my breath. It was so cold and delicious. I took the other bottle to Lucas who was standing at the window looking up the street.

"What are you looking at?"

He turned around and I handed him the water. "Nothing. Just making sure that guy is gone. I'm gonna hit the shower. Care to join me?"

"No thanks," I said nonchalantly. "I'll wait my turn."

"Suit yourself."

I turned to look out the window and drank more of my water. I imagined Lucas in the other room, naked and wet, lathered up with soap, washing the salty sweat off his strong body. It was all I could do to stop myself from getting in that shower with him.

I looked up the street and saw the man was gone. I guessed he must have been waiting for someone. I finished my water and went back to the fridge for another one. I heard the shower turn off and a minute later Lucas emerged, soaking wet with nothing but a towel wrapped around his waist. My stomach ached and I could feel heat rising from my hips up to my face. I turned away and went for my duffle bag, hoping he would go to his room to get dressed. What was I waiting for? Go attack him! The devil in me was loud. Shut up you bitch! I cursed back at her.

"I think I'll just head back to my place," I said, fumbling with my bag.

"Why? Don't go, I was gonna order some food. It's still early."

"Okay fine, but go get dressed and I'll just take a quick shower."

"The bathroom's all yours. Chinese okay?"

"Yep…that's fine."

I heard the door to his bedroom close and I let out a sigh of relief. It had been a long time since I had dated but I was pretty sure I didn't remember this part. I wished I hadn't asked Lamb to get information about Lucas. I wished I had just taken the time to get to know him on my own. But when I thought about it, what I knew wasn't really much more than what Lucas already knew. He knew his parents had been killed and he seemed to have gotten past that. But it was the bigger stuff, like why his parents were killed and by whom. I was worried that he wouldn't forgive himself if he realized that it was his job that had got them killed. But was that the reason? Lamb was just guessing. But it couldn't just be a huge coincidence that they had been killed right after his cover was blown.

No matter how much I tried to convince myself otherwise, I knew I had to do the right thing and tell him what I knew. I grabbed my bag and stomped off to the shower. I was worried that he'd blocked all of the painful things out for a reason, so what would happen when he found out? But maybe I wasn't giving him enough credit. Or maybe I was just scared that when I did tell him he wouldn't want to have anything to do with me.

Chapter Six

So which one are you going to?" Lucas was sprawled across my bed watching me pack.

"Oh, we have a house on Ocracoke Island in North Carolina. We've had that house since I can remember. But since my mom died, my father and I haven't been back."

"Really...why not?"

"Well, we just forgot about it I guess. After she died I went to boarding school. We never really talked about it after that.

"I'm sorry."

"Me too. My mom loved the ocean...even wanted to live there. But with my father's work there was no way that was going to happen. He bought the house to pacify her. She took me there a few times a year and two months every summer while my father worked. It will be good to get back."

"Not for me. I'm going to miss you," he said, pulling me onto the bed with him. He kissed me passionately, his hands pulling in my hair. I could feel my blood begin to heat up, but I pulled away and sat up.

"What's the matter?"

"Nothing, I just need to finish packing this stuff."

"Come on, Jen, you've obviously been avoiding this. Be honest with me."

My stomach twisted at the word honest. "I'm not avoiding you. I don't want to make love and leave for a week. When the time is right, I promise." I leaned in and touched his cheek.

"Fine." He flopped onto his back and locked his hands behind his head.

"You know you could always come with me." Why the hell had I just said that?

"Don't tempt me. As much as I would love to, I can't; I have work. How about when you get back I'll make you a candlelit dinner?"

"That sounds nice." I smiled.

"You'd better call me when you get there. I'll be lonely here without you."

I sat on the bed next to him and he leaned up onto his elbow.

"I'll miss you too." I wanted him to change his mind and come with me. I wanted to say screw what I know so we could just get on with our relationship already.

"I hope you know I'm mostly kidding with you. In all seriousness, though…" he paused…"I hope I fit into your life somewhere."

I took his hand and entwined our fingers together, surprised that he would doubt my feelings for him.

"Meeting you came very unexpectedly." I chose my words carefully. "I know it's only been a few weeks, but I feel like I've known you a lot longer. I didn't know what was missing from my life until I met you, and I thought it would be a hell of a lot scarier than this, but it's not. You make me feel comfortable and safe and I don't want that to change."

I stressed every day about what his reaction would be when he found out that I knew about his past. I had intruded on his life without his permission. It made me sad every time I imagined him being angry with me and leaving. But I was going to tell him whether he thanked me or left me.

"I just want you to know that this isn't something casual for me. You're in my life now." His eyes were steady on mine as he touched my cheek. His palm felt warm.

I leaned in and kissed him softly. "You've been on my mind ever since we met in the diner."

I fiddled with my hair as I watched him lick his bottom lip then bite it. He grinned playfully as he looked at me under hooded eyes. Uh oh! He pulled me onto the bed and I squealed under his tickles, begging him to stop. He finally relented and leaned over me with a boyish smile on his face.

"Are you sure you don't want to come with me?" I said, catching my breath.

"I'm sure."

At the airport, we stood with our arms around each other's waists, leaning our foreheads together. He was clean-shaven and smelled spicy. I put my head into his neck and inhaled softly then kissed his ear lightly. He took me by my shoulders and kissed me deeply. The announcement came for the final boarding call. Feeling breathless, I promised him I would call if I got into any trouble and walked to the plane.

The flight to Norfolk, Virginia was short. I picked up my rental car and began the drive through the warm weather to the coast. I recognized some of the busy areas when I drove through the Outer Banks in North Carolina and smiled as the locals waved as though we were old friends. People walked around in bathing suits and families rode bikes. It was perfect; just what I needed. The drive down Highway 12 was boring and I had about a half hour until I reached Cape Hatteras where I would catch the ferry to Ocracoke.

I pulled into a gas station to fill up before getting on the ferry. I would still have forty minutes to kill while I crossed the Pamlico Sound and arrive in Ocracoke. I decided to get some gossip magazines and snacks to help pass the time. I was daydreaming about being at the house, remembering my mom, when my phone rang. I was sure it was Lucas.

"Hello?"

"Hey Jen."

"Oh, hey Lamb. Is everything okay?"

"Yeah, sure, everything is fine. I was just calling to check in with you. I haven't talked to you since I saw you a few weeks ago."

"Everything's fine on my end, but thanks for calling."

"Was that Lucas Benjamin you were with the other night?"

I rolled my eyes and sighed. "Um, yes it was actually."

"Is he a client of yours?"

"Why do you ask, Lamb?"

"Look, I know I don't normally intrude with cases you work on. To be perfectly frank with you honey, I'm a little worried."

"Well, there's nothing to worry about."

"I'm not sure if you're aware or not, Jen, but the people he was involved with were a serious bunch of men. He may not remember what happened to him but one day he just might and all hell could break loose. I don't like the thought of you being in the middle of that. I love you like a daughter, Jen. I know you're a smart cookie, but just be careful."

Lamb was sweet. He had been more like a father to me than my real father ever was. It had turned into such a habit for me to call Lamb instead of my father I didn't even give it a second thought any more. "I'm aware of his situation Lamb. Thank you for your concern about it though. It means a lot that you worry about me."

"I know things with your dad aren't always great. But he loves you and only wants the best for you. Maybe you should tell him about this new case you're working."

Why was he bringing up my father? "My father is retired remember? What I do with my cases is my business."

"All right then, have a good week off. Where ya headed anyway?"

"I'm going to the house at the coast. I need to be around my mom right now."

"All by yourself?"

"Yes…all by myself. I'm a big girl, remember?"

"Okay, girlie, you enjoy yourself, and don't be a stranger, huh?"

"I won't. Bye."

Lamb knew more about my life than my father did. My father hadn't even said goodbye to me before I left, even though we'd had a lunch meeting. I'd assured him that I wasn't leaving any loose ends and that I would be reachable by phone. He hadn't even asked where I was going. Just as well. All the questions Lamb was suddenly asking were weird though.

I pulled off the ferry into Ocracoke just before five and stopped at a small store to pick up a few groceries for dinner and breakfast, intending to go to a supermarket the next day.

The house looked just as I remembered. My father had been keeping the place maintained, I could tell. Since we hadn't been to the house in so long I had expected it to look run down and unkempt. But the grass was green and meticulously mowed. The two big rhododendron bushes were blooming bright pink under the front windows. It looked bright and cheerful.

Inside, everything was exactly the same; the oversized furniture in the living room, the picnic style table in the soft yellow-colored kitchen, the ships in bottles on the bookcase, even the smell of lavender that my mother had loved so much. I wandered around, feeling good about my decision to come here, letting my fingers drape across the back of the sofa. I saw a picture of me and my mother on an end table and realized there were no pictures of my father anywhere. I couldn't shake a strange feeling that someone had been there recently, but that didn't make any sense.

I made myself a peanut butter and jelly sandwich and a pot of coffee. After I ate I went outside to the beach and walked for a while, breathing in the ocean air. It felt good to be away from the city and to be in a place that held special memories for me. I searched for shells like my mother and I used to do together. I found a few favorites to take home. When I got back to the house I was feeling energized and refreshed and I decided to call Lucas.

"How was your trip?"

"It was pretty uneventful. Now that I'm here and I've done all the things a person should do in order to relax, I feel sorta lonely. I wish you were here."

"Trust me; if I were there you wouldn't be getting much rest."

I smiled. I knew he was trying to lighten my mood and it was working, so I decided to play along. "Oh really…and what would you be doing if you were here right now?"

"How about I just show you when I see you again?"

"I plan to hold you to that." I heard what sounded like an announcement over an intercom. "Hey, where are you?"

"Oh, ah, I'm just about to get on the subway. I was downtown and didn't want to blow the money on a cab to get home."

"Oh, okay." I thought that was strange since Lucas never took the subway, but I didn't press the issue.

We talked for a little while longer and said our goodbyes. I had trouble falling asleep, thinking about what Lamb had said on the phone. I worried more about how Lucas would react when I finally told him about his past. Would he be really hurt? What would become of the two of us? I couldn't keep what I knew a secret from him. My story, the one I'd been living the past four years, was going to change. It was time for me to rewrite it.

I woke up early and it was raining so I put off going to the supermarket as I had planned. I was lazy most of the morning and didn't even get dressed. I was sitting on a chair looking out at the ocean, drinking a cup of coffee when I heard a knock at the front door. Who could that be? Maybe it was a neighbor checking to see who was there. I didn't even know how long it had been since anyone had been to the house.

I got up and went to the door. I stood on tip toe to look out the peep hole and saw Lucas standing there, soaking wet. I opened the door nervously, worried that something was wrong. Did he know what I'd done? Was he there to confront me?

"What are you doing here? Come in!"

He stepped into the house and I closed the door.

"I had some good news and thought I'd surprise you."

"How did you find the house?" I went to the bathroom and brought a towel back for him.

"I'm a detective, remember?" he said with a grin. "I got a call after you left and then practically left right behind you. I was actually at the airport when you called last night."

"A call? From who?"

"Did you just wake up?"

I looked down at myself. "No, I've been up all morning. I'm on vacation so why get dressed? I can't believe you came all the way here. Stop stalling…what's this good news?"

He rubbed the towel through his hair, making it stick up. He left the towel draped around his shoulders and held onto the ends. "I got the security job I interviewed for a couple weeks ago. I quit the museum and I start the new job next week. I had nothing to do until then so I decided to come and tell you in person. I know I should have called first, in fact I felt uneasy about coming here as soon as I got off the ferry." He rubbed the back of his neck.

"How did you even get here?" I asked, peering out the window. There was a red sedan in the driveway.

"I rented a car and I'm about to get in it and head back."

"No, please don't go." He took my breath away. He had no idea how sexy he was. He could've been on set for a modeling shoot. His hair was wet and water was dripping off the curls around his neck. I could see the outline of his chest through the damp shirt sticking to his skin. I leaned in and gave him a tight hug. "I'm really glad to see you."

"I'm glad too. I wasn't sure how you would react…" His words trailed off as he looked at me intently. "But I took my chances anyway."

He pulled me to him and gave me a long, passionate kiss. It felt so good to be in his arms again, feeling safe and connected to him. I grabbed the back of his neck and pulled him into a tighter kiss, feeling passion run through me like wild fire. It was unlike me to be so wanting so I pulled away. "I'm sorry; I don't know what came over me."

"Don't apologize. I enjoyed every minute of it. You don't have to stop." He took a step closer and ran a hand down my arm, sending chills over my skin.

I looked at him and ran my tongue over my bottom lip. His tousled hair, his chiseled jaw with a new dusting of stubble, the muscles outlined by his wet shirt; it was driving me crazy.

Before I knew it my hands were in his hair and I was kissing him again. I moaned slightly with my mouth against his. It had been so long since I had been touched by a man, in any kind of way, and it felt so good. He turned me round and pushed me up against the wall and started kissing my neck. Everything below my waist started to ache.

"I've wanted this for so long," he said into my neck.

I moaned with pleasure. And just like a douse of cold water being dumped on me I heard Lamb's voice in my head: He may not remember what happened to him but one day he just might and all hell could break loose.

"Stop Lucas," I said, pushing against his chest.

He stopped kissing my neck and looked at me with his mouth slightly open, eyebrows pushed together. "What's the matter?"

"Nothing…I just don't want to rush into anything is all." I slipped away from the space between him and the wall. I started smoothing my shirt out, trying to push the want out of me. I took a deep breath and blinked a few times, composing myself.

"What are you talking about? We obviously both feel the same way about each other…don't we?" His question trailed off as doubt surrounded us like a fog.

"Yes, we definitely feel the same way about each other." I tried to think of a logical reason why it wouldn't make sense to make love. "I guess I feel like we're still getting to know each other and I don't want to ruin anything." Yeah, that should stick for now. I chewed on the inside of my cheek nervously, waiting for him to respond.

"Is this because of my past?" He ran a hand through his hair. "I knew I shouldn't have told you all that shit about me. It's probably for the best anyway - I don't want you exposed to anything because of me. Maybe I should just go then. I'm sorry I came here unannounced…I'm seeing now that it was a bad idea." He took the towel that was still around his shoulders and held it out to me.

"No, you don't have to go." I took the towel from him. I twisted it, hoping to wring strength from it. "Please stay."

He stood with his arms folded, looking at me. I could tell he was torn about what to do. I put my hand on his cheek and smiled softly. "This has nothing to do with your past or what happened to you. It's been so long since I've been in a relationship I'm not sure what I'm doing any more. I just want to take it slow, that's all, I promise."

He raised an eyebrow. "Are you sure?"

"Yes, I'm absolutely sure. I would love the company."

"Well, okay. You are definitely a hard one to figure out, you know that?"

I mustered up my best fake laugh. "Why don't I make us something to eat? Oh wait…" I said, frowning. "I never went to get groceries."

"I'll run to the store."

"It's pouring."

"You stay here and I'll be back before you know it."

"Okay, if you're sure, that would be great." I smiled.

I gave him some quick directions and he went to a store nearby. I took a shower, got dressed and turned on some music. I found a few candles but couldn't find anything to light them with. I looked through drawers and cabinets but had no luck, so I went to the linen closet, remembering there were baskets of odds and ends in there. I looked around the shelves, still not finding a lighter. I kicked a box that was sticking out under the last shelf. Ow! I bent down to rub my toe and saw the box was labeled 'Patricia'. Mom.

Curious, I sat on the floor and pulled the box out of the closet. I slowly took the lid off. I fingered through a few photos and saw that at the bottom were some of her favorite books. I smiled as I ran a finger across a big starfish, remembering the day she found it while we walked together on the beach. I noticed there were other boxes as well so I pulled another one out. The next one was full of notebooks and journals. I had no idea she even kept a journal. I took one from the top and flipped to the last page. The date was the year she died. "Phillip is out of town again this week. I took Jennifer to the Central Park Zoo…" My heart started to pound as the memory of my mother and me at the zoo flooded my brain. My hands were shaking so I slapped the book shut; I wasn't ready to read that yet.

There were a few more boxes in the back of the closet. I pushed the others aside and pulled one out labeled 'confidential.' I took the lid off; it was full of files. I chose a random folder and saw that it was a client file from work. Why were there work files here? I fingered through the rest of the box and pulled out another one that caught my eye, noticing it was a different color to the rest. It was full of transcripts. I scanned through the top pages and when I got half way through I paused. 'That's when

I found out Josh was really a cop. But I had nothing to do with that fire or his parents. Maybe karma got to him for messing with the wrong kind of people.' Josh must have been Lucas's undercover name and it dawned on me that I was reading the transcript about his parents' murders. My heart started pounding and I tried to steady my hands so I could keep reading. I flipped the file back to the front trying to look for a name. I found it; Vance Wallace. His name had been in the news a lot back in New York. At the end of the transcripts it was documented that there wasn't enough evidence to charge the suspect for the fire. I closed the file and kept it in my lap. My father had represented the very man Lucas was trying to bust while undercover? The revelation was unfathomable. How could that be? The police must have arrested Vance Wallace for the murders. And my father got him off?

The front door opened.

"I got tons of great stuff," Lucas said from the kitchen. I heard bags dropping on the counter. "Jen? Where are you?"

I quickly put the file back and pushed all the boxes into the closet and closed the door. I went to the kitchen to see Lucas unloading a bottle of wine and some kind of cheese from one of the bags. A red grape rolled off the counter and onto the floor, coming to rest at my feet.

"There you are." He looked at me and stopped what he was doing. He came over and took my shoulders. "Hey, are you alright? You look like you've just seen a ghost."

I hugged him and buried my head in his shoulder, starting to cry. I was overwhelmed with everything I knew. His parents, my father…it was too much.

He rubbed my back lightly. "Hey, it's okay. What happened?"

I didn't know what to say. I didn't know where to start. "I found a box with some of my mother's things…" I began.

"Oh Jen, I'm sorry. It must be hard being here without her."

I pulled out of his arms and wiped my face, trying to collect myself a bit. "No, it's not that. We need to talk." I took his hand, led him to the living room and sat with him on the sofa. "I have to tell you something very serious and I want you to sit here until I'm finished, okay?"

"Okay…"

"Do you remember when we met in the diner the first time?"

"Mm hm."

"Well, the next day I asked Lamb, the man you met while we were on our first date, if he would get your full name and address for me."

"Why didn't you just ask me? What would you want that for anyway?"

"I don't have a good answer for that. I saw you sitting on the bench at the bus stop every day and I couldn't stop wondering." I looked down into my hands, feeling ashamed.

"What would knowing my name and address tell you anyway?"

"That's not really the point right now."

"You mean there's more?" he asked wide-eyed. "Please, continue. I can't wait." He folded his arms, his spine stiff.

"Lamb recognized your name from the media. Apparently your parents' death was big news."

He put his hands up, stopping me. "Whoa…what does any of this have to do with my parents?"

I took a deep breath.

"Before they were killed you were working undercover. Your cover was somehow blown." I waited.

"And…?"

"You were working…"

"Yeah I was working to bust the biggest drug gang in the city! How on earth did you - "

I waited, ashamed. He didn't say anything but looked right at me. His eyes were wide and his mouth was open slightly. He stood up and ran his hands through his wet hair, pacing. He stopped and looked at me. "Are you happy? Are you?" He threw his hands in the air. "I have to get outta here."

Oh shit! He opened the door and disappeared outside.

"Lucas, wait!" I yelled through the pouring rain, following him.

He turned around abruptly and faced me, making me flinch. "So all that shit I told you in my apartment that night…you let me go on and on about being in the hospital when you already knew! You just wanted to know why I sat at the bus stop, is that it? Did you get your answer Jennifer? Are you satisfied?"

"No, Lucas, please. After we started getting to know each other I didn't care about that anymore."

"So what…this all started out as a little pet project for you? Find out why the lonely man sits and stares all day?" He pushed his wet hair out of his eyes. "You've been leading me on, waiting until you get your answer, is that it? Make sure I'm not some crazy freak? Well, I'm sorry if I don't measure up to your expectations. You've certainly put on one hell of a Broadway show with me the past couple of weeks." He turned to leave but stopped to face me again. "Why are you telling me now anyway?" His voice was clipped with anger.

I had to tell him the rest. I was scared and frustrated and I blamed my father for it.

"Because my father got him off!" I said, pounding my closed fists at my side. I began sobbing.

"Wait…got who off…you don't mean…" Lucas whispered, shaking his head in disbelief.

I couldn't look at him anymore. I wish I had never found that file. I forced myself to meet his eyes.

"It's true. My father was responsible for getting the man who killed your parents acquitted."

The only sound was of the rain and it had soaked us both. I wanted to wrap my arms around him and tell him how sorry I was.

"There was a box behind my mother's things in the closet. I thought it was just more of her stuff, but when I looked through it I found files from work."

As if he was no longer listening to me, he reached into his back pocket and pulled out his wallet. He took something out of it and, after staring at it for a moment, he looked at me with disbelief in his eyes. "You work at Monroe, Lambert, and Tate." It was my business card. "But…but you're last name is Callahan..." He turned his back to me and ran a hand through his hair. He faced me again. "Phillip Monroe is your father?"

"Lucas, please…."

"Stop, stop, stop!" He put his hands to his forehead and squeezed his eyes shut. "I can't listen to this. I have to be alone."

He got into his car. I stood there in the rain with my arms wrapped tightly around myself, shivering as I watched the tail lights disappear. I turned and walked to the house, looking back a couple of times at the road, hoping he would come back.

I changed clothes and towel dried my hair and went to the kitchen to make coffee. My mind was racing and I was sure his was too. What would he do now? Where had he gone? He was so angry at me right now. So much had happened in only an hour with finding those boxes and talking to Lucas, I was both physically and mentally exhausted. I tried to figure out what to do but my mind was blank. One minute everything had been fine and then it was all crashing down around me. I feared our relationship had just gone up in flames.

∂∘ઽ

I must have dozed off on the couch because I was startled awake by the front door opening and closing. I sat up, trying to focus in the dim light. Lucas was walking into the living room. He sat down and I wanted to rush over to him, hug him, kiss him, ask him if he was okay, but I didn't feel certain about anything anymore.

"I was worried about you," I whispered. "Are you alright?"

"I'm sorry I took off like that." He ran a hand through his damp hair. "I really needed to be alone for a while. I found a tavern down the road and sat and had a beer."

"I'm glad you came back." I hesitated. "I'm sorry I didn't tell you what I knew sooner."

"It's okay. I'm sorry I blew up before. It's just…I hate that you know all this shit about me. I got my parents killed and now you could be in danger…it's just a lot to take in, you know?"

"Lucas," I said, fighting back tears, "the truth about you is beautiful. I'm the one who hates that you know the truth about me and my father."

His eyes met mine with sadness. "I've felt like a piece of me was missing for a long time, but since I met you I'm being put back together again."

"I wasn't trying to lead you on or lie to you, I'm so sorry. I never expected to have feelings for you…I never planned any of this."

"I know, and I'm sorry for what I said earlier. I don't like thinking about my parents…all it does is remind me that I couldn't save then and can't remember that night. In fact, I don't know if I would have ever remembered anything if it weren't for you, so thank you."

"Wait, what? What do you remember?"

"While I was at the tavern I was thinking of the dream I always have…you know, the one with those two guys coming out of the court house and laughing at me? It suddenly dawned on me…I know exactly who those two guys are. They were Vance Wallace and his attorney. I was sitting on the bench when they came out all full of themselves after it was determined there wasn't enough evidence to try Wallace on a drug charge. It was right after that that I went undercover. I don't remember anything else though."

As I listened, I pictured the men walking out of the court house, knowing that one of the faces of the two men belonged to my father. I was ashamed. Lucas knew who my father was and had been sitting on that bench all this time because he had been there before, determined to make sure one day Vance Wallace went to prison. I was furious. Vance Wallace had been released, Lucas had gone undercover, his parents had been killed, and yet my father had protected Vance again.

"So what happens now?" I asked.

"I don't have much of a game plan in mind right now, Jen. What I do know for sure is that I don't want you involved in this in any way." He leaned forward onto his knees and looked right at me. "Wallace isn't somebody to mess with, him or his people. I have a feeling my amnesia is what's kept me alive this long. If he were to find out I'm involved with you, I wouldn't doubt the first thing he'd try to do is to get rid of the both of us. I want you as far away from that as possible."

My heart sank. The idea of something happening to Lucas made me feel sick to my stomach. Although what he said made perfect sense, hell, I would have given the same advice to any client, it didn't change the fact that I wanted to help him somehow. The 'how' was the hard part.

"Look, I know you want to protect me and I appreciate that, I really do. I deal with bottom feeders all the time so I know how to take care of myself. There has to be something I can do to help. Maybe I can have Lamb…."

"Just stop right there. There's no way I want you involved. If Wallace found out, who knows what he'd do. And what about your father - what happens when he finds out who your new boyfriend is? He might already know."

I considered that for a moment. If my father did know that I was involved with Lucas, wouldn't he confront me with it; tell me it isn't a good idea? Ever since he'd gotten back from California he'd seemed even more distant than usual. And the way he'd reacted when I overslept that day and blew up about me being unreachable wasn't his style either. Maybe he knew something and was afraid to tell me. I wondered if my father was confiding in Lamb and that was why Lamb had been checking up on me so much. Maybe someone even knew that Lucas was at the beach house with me. I was beginning to feel frightened.

"I'll deal with my father and figure things out on that end," I said, trying to hide my fear. "But what I don't want is to lose you, Lucas. You're the first good thing that's happened in my life in so long. I know that's incredibly selfish of me after all you've been through, but dammit, I can't help it!"

"Hey, don't get all ahead of yourself just yet, okay?" He took my hand. "I don't want to lose you either, Jen. But the thought of what happened to my parents happening to you...it's just inconceivable to me. You're all I have left in this world. Keeping you safe is what matters most to me."

"Whichever way you look at it, I'm involved one way or the other. I'm on the lawyer side or your side."

"I'd rather you be on the lawyer side for now. At least if Wallace sees you as an ally then he won't give you a second thought. You'd be a pawn if he knew about us." He stood up and pulled me into his arms. "Come here." He held me close. "I can't bear the thought of something happening to you." He squeezed me tighter. "You're home to me. That means you stay out of all this shit and let me handle it."

We hugged for a while and I cried softly into his shoulder.

"Come on, let's go to bed."

We walked to the bedroom and lay together for a long time, not saying a word. I lay on his chest, thinking about my mother and how much I wished she was still there. She had always taken care of me when I was hurt or troubled. She'd been gone for so long and my father had never filled that role. I'd learned how to take of myself. Hearing Lucas say how he felt about me was foreign but at the same time it was what I needed; like air in my lungs. And I liked it...I liked it a lot.

Chapter Seven

The next morning Lucas went back to the city. It was hard for me to say goodbye to him, and his final kiss lingered on my lips for the rest of the morning. My mind was consumed with thoughts that he was in trouble and that something bad could happen at any moment. I had promised I wouldn't call him for a few days unless it was an emergency, would try to keep a low profile.

I decided to head back to the closet and get the box of files out again. I needed to get a better look at them and see if I could figure out a way to help Lucas. I just couldn't sit back and watch, especially when I had a lot of information right under my nose.

I gently pushed my mother's boxes out of the way with bitterness that my father had used them to hide any possible impropriety with the Vance Wallace case. I couldn't help feeling that my father was up to something. If there wasn't anything to hide, why hide the files at all?

I took the box of files marked 'confidential' to the living room and sat on the floor. I opened it and began slowly taking out files one at a time. A typical client file should have contained a copy of the statute describing a charge, the courtroom assignment, a profile of the judge, the best approaches to defending the case, and the possible sentencing alternatives. I read each one carefully and made notes. I made it through half of the box and I stopped, wondering why those files were at the beach house. The charges on these clients were typical; mostly drug related, but a couple involved weapons and robbery.

I finally made it to the end and I had to get up and stretch. I had been sitting there for almost two hours. I was tired and hungry so I made a sandwich and brought that and a glass of milk into the living room. While I sat quietly eating, a thought popped into my head. I grabbed my piece of scrap paper and reread an earlier thought I had written out. No common names, dad the only connection. I looked at the first couple of files I had started with and sure enough, I found a similarity. All of these clients had a California address.

I took out the Vance Wallace transcripts, wondering why the file was in a box full of unimportant ones. Why wouldn't this be kept in my father's office under lock and key? I read it over a dozen times looking for some loophole but there wasn't anything. My father was no dummy, so what little he allowed Vance to actually say was simple. My new focus was how Vance came to be represented by my father.

I heard my phone ding. telling me I had a text message. It was from Lucas.

"Hey…made it 2 Virginia. Just wanted 2 check in w u & tell u I miss u."

"Hey…happy to hear from you. I miss you too."

"I'll b in touch in a few days. G'nite!"

"Night."

It was hard to leave the conversation with just that, but I did. I was tired and decided to call it quits for the day. I nuked a microwave dinner and took it out to the deck and sat for a while watching the ocean until it was chilly and dark.

As usual I woke just before dawn with a pounding headache. I still had three days left of my so-called vacation and I was far from relaxed. So much for 'getting away from it all.' After making coffee, I walked into the living room with its mess of paper work and files. I saw my notes and sat down to look them over. Wondering about California again my thoughts were distracted. Daddy had been there many times to 'smooth things over' as he called it, but he'd never told me what actually needed to be smoothed over.

I got out my computer to start a search online. My fingers sat resting on the keys as I tried to figure out what, exactly, I wanted to search for. A name…I'd start with someone who lived there. I grabbed a random file marked with the client name 'William Bradshaw.' The first result was a website address for a computer manufacturing company. There was a picture of the COO, William Bradshaw, and a description of him and the company. I scanned the article. 'Born and raised….,' yeah, yeah, 'built the company from the ground up….,' 'wife and 2 children…,'' nothing was really all that interesting. The company was based in California with satellite offices all over the U.S. I sat back and thought about this man as a client. He had been arrested for possession of cocaine several times and it looked like my father had got him off every time. I couldn't help but wonder how my father, a lawyer based in New York, came to be this man's defense attorney.

The rest of the day I spent searching the client names on the internet and making notes on each of them, making my own mini client files. The majority of clients had large businesses from manufacturing to shipping. The rest had small businesses and were restaurant owners and landlords. There seemed to be no thread common to all of them, except for the fact that they were all men who lived in California, and had my father listed as their attorney. One file caught my eye when I realized my father wasn't listed as the attorney. Manny Fiori owned a small grocery store in San Diego. It was a file that was filled out by hand with this man's name, address, phone numbers and business information. He had no charges for arrest, so what was my father's involvement?

By just after three in the afternoon I was famished and needed to clear my head. I made a cheese omelet and a cup of hot tea. My thoughts were all over the place from worrying about what was happening back in New York with Lucas, thinking about my father and wondering what he'd been hiding. What would Mom have told me to do right now? I knew right away what my next step had to be; I had to go to California and see what I could find out.

I went to my computer, bringing up flight information to California. I booked a morning flight for the next day. My cell phone began ringing - my father. Did he know I'd found the files? Did he know I was going to California? I put my phone down and began twirling my hair. Calm down, Jennifer. How could he possibly know any of that stuff? He must have been calling about a client which meant I needed to call him back right away. I had promised I would be reachable and I didn't want to spark any suspicion.

I wasn't surprised when he answered on the first ring.

"Hello, Jennifer, how is your trip going?" I could hear he was typing on his computer as he spoke.

"The trip is fine. I was…just in the shower and couldn't get to my phone right away. Is everything alright…any client trouble?" I cringed at how flustered I was. I hoped he couldn't hear it in my voice.

"No, everything is fine here. I just wanted to make sure you were finding everything you needed at the beach house."

He knew where I was. He must have found out from Lamb, that's the only way he could possibly have known. I took a deep breath and sat up straight, composing myself as if I were in court. "It's been great being here again. Aside from the rain the first couple of days, I'm seeing why Mom loved it here so much. The ocean is beautiful and the house is exactly as I remember it."

I heard him whisper something, to his assistant, no doubt. He was clearly not paying that much attention to his conversation with me. "Yes, well, your mother loved that house and I couldn't bring myself to rent it out, thinking about strangers being around all of your mother's favorite things."

I looked around the living room and knew exactly what he meant. It surprised me that my father had any kind of emotional connection at all with this house. Maybe he did miss Mom and he put on a façade for everyone. To be perceived as weak would be unacceptable to him.

"I know what you mean. Being here brings back a lot of memories. I should come here more often."

"You go whenever you like. I only wish you would have told me you were going there. I would have had the cleaning lady come to have it ready for you."

"I'm sorry. The subject never came up. To be honest it was just a spur of the moment decision and I didn't even consider that you might be renting it out. We don't really talk enough." I felt a wave of guilt wash over me. But it was true; he was my father and I still loved him. Every day I hoped would finally be the day we would connect and be family, not colleagues.

It was silent for a moment and I heard him sigh softly. "I know I haven't been the best father to you Jennifer, and I'm sorry for that. I did the best I could with you, but your mother was the one who always knew better than me what you needed. After she…..after she passed….I didn't know how to be a father to you without her. I knew how close you and your mother were and I got scared you would go down a path that would lead you nowhere fast. So I did the only thing I knew, and that was to try and keep you safe. Working with you has given me the opportunity to see you grow into a beautiful, smart woman with a natural ability as a lawyer. I'm very proud of you Jennifer. I know I don't say it much, but I mean it. You're my daughter and I love you."

I felt a tear roll down my cheek but I wanted to hold back the sobs with everything I had in me. I didn't want him to know I was crying. I had been waiting my whole life to hear him say just a fraction of what he had just said. I almost wished he was there so I could hug him and tell him how much I missed him. I blinked and caught a glimpse of the files that were strewn all over the place in front of me, bringing me back down to Earth.

I wiped my cheeks with the back of my hand and cleared my throat. If we were ever to connect, it would have to be without lies. All the information I had found tucked away in the house was there for a reason. That reason would be something I'd have to find out for myself. Because no matter how much I wanted to delude myself that he was calling to see how I was doing, my gut told me he just wanted to make sure his secrets were still safely hidden.

"I love you too Daddy. That really means a lot, thank you."

"Well….I'll let you get back….to whatever you're doing then."

"Okay, thanks for calling. I'll see you on Monday."

"When you return the two of us will have dinner. Tell Karen so you don't forget."

And just like that the soft-hearted man who was just confessing his feelings was gone. I had to laugh to myself. He had confirmed what my gut had been telling me. "I'll have to check my schedule when I get back. I'll let you know."

"I'm sure anything you have on your schedule can be changed so there shouldn't be any need. But, if you insist, go ahead and check. Enjoy the rest of your time then. Goodbye Jennifer."

"Goodbye Daddy."

I slumped back onto the couch and nervously twirled my hair. I had spent most of my time with my mother when I was young, never thinking there was anything wrong with the fact that my father wasn't around much. I thought again about what he had said about the house and how meaningful it must be to him to keep it a place that was still just hers. Maybe he wasn't the cold-hearted bastard I thought he was after all. Maybe he really just didn't know how to be a parent because he'd left that up to my mother. He had said he molded me into what I am today so he could keep me close and make sure I was safe. How could I be angry at him for that? He may have kept me from doing something really stupid with my life. I hated to think I would be that stupid but I supposed I had proved I was all during college when I hadn't cared what happened to me. I had never thought about it. But my father must have.

I wondered what my father would think of Lucas. He would respect the fact that he had been a police officer, doing the right thing in society. If things had been different, if Lucas hadn't almost been killed by a man that my father represented, I would have already introduced them to each other. Out of all the millions of people in New York City, why had my father had to represent Vance Wallace? That seemed to be the million dollar question and I still intended to find out the answer.

I Googled the name Vance Wallace. I chose the first result that came up and was immediately blown away. There was a picture of a well-dressed man in a dark grey suit wearing a pink silk tie. His eyes were dark and cold and I got chills, feeling as though he was staring right at me. His chin was square and his jaw was locked in a serious expression. I was finally seeing his face; the face of a murderer. There was an article about his business; his shipping business…in California.

Shit, none of it was making sense. I was frustrated and wanted to help Lucas so badly. I got the file out for Manny Fiori. I would begin my investigation into all of this at his grocery store. Starting someplace small seemed to make sense and would probably keep me off the radar.

Chapter Eight

The next morning I left at 6 A.M. so I could be in Virginia for my flight to California by two. I had hardly slept the night before. I had had a dream about Vance Wallace killing Lucas on the steps of the court house while I watched from the bus stop. The irony wasn't lost on me but it just made me more determined to find something out that would help Lucas to put Vance Wallace away once and for all. I hadn't spoken to Lucas since he had texted me the day before and I longed to call him just to be able to hear his voice. But he would ask me what I was doing and I wouldn't have been able to lie to him. He would have been furious if he'd known I was snooping around in California.

My first step when I got to California would be to visit the grocery store and see what it was like. Was it busy? How big was it? What were the owners like? I needed a starting point and that was the best thing I could come up with.

I arrived in Virginia at 12:45 with a little bit of time before my flight. I decided to have coffee and something to eat before I boarded the plane. I went to one of the Starbucks inside the airport, found a quiet table and began looking at the Sun Journal newspaper. I heard my phone ding, telling me I had a text message.

Hey, just wanted 2 C how u R doing.

Oh shit, it was Lucas. Calm down, Jennifer; just tell him you're fine.

I've been thinking about you! I'm fine...how are you?

Please don't ask me what I'm doing, please don't ask me what I'm doing.

Things aren't any different here. Frustrated. Can't wait 2 C u!

Oh no, there was no new news about Vance. Well, hopefully I could change all of that.

I'm sorry about that. One thing at a time for now. Be home in a couple of days. We'll talk then.

OK, b safe. Call if u need me.

My determination shifted into overdrive. I couldn't imagine what I would find but I was hopeful nonetheless.

కావ్

My flight was long and tiring, especially since I hadn't slept well the night before. I was sat next to a crying baby the entire time and his mother was having a difficult time soothing him. I felt bad for her but was also ready to be off that plane.

Outside the airport I was hugged by a cool breeze. The sun was shining and white clouds dotted the blue sky. I took a cleansing breath in and exhaled slowly, feeling some of the stress escape me. I hooked my overnight bag onto my shoulder and hailed a cab, asking the driver to take me to West Cedar Market, Little Italy in San Diego. He knew right where it was and we were there in about twenty minutes.

The driver pulled up alongside the curb right in front of the store. I sat looking out the window, taking an inventory of the store and its surroundings. The building was small, made of red brick and located on the corner with two iron tables and chairs in front. There was a faded red awning over the front door that had an 'OPEN' sign hanging from it. There was nothing out of the ordinary about the place. I decided to get out.

"Can you please wait while I run into the store?" I asked the driver.

"Sorry, ma'am, but I can't stay parked here at the curb."

I looked back at the store wondering if I should risk being dropped off, not knowing where I was or where I was going next. Things aren't any different here. Frustrated. Lucas's words from his last text reminded me I was there for a reason and I intended to find out something. I paid the driver, thanked him and got out.

I walked into the small store and immediately felt a rush of cold. There were small isles filled with minimal amounts of grocery items and in the back was a deli counter for sliced meats and sandwiches. The delicious smell of fresh bread filled the small space and my stomach growled. I began browsing around, pretending to be shopping. I heard a door close at the back of the store and a heavy-set, short woman in her mid-forties with curly black hair walked out from behind the deli counter. She was wiping her hands on the bottom of her white apron. She spotted me and smiled sweetly.

"Can I help you?"

"Um…no, I don't think so." I searched for something intelligent to say but I was so nervous. "I heard this was a great place for a sandwich." What? What was I talking about?

I heard the door close again and a tall man with pocked skin, a goatee and a grim expression on his face came out. His eyebrows were knitted together. He put his hands on his hips and said something in Italian to the woman. She shrugged her shoulders and answered him back. The man directed his gaze back to me.

"I've never seen you before around the neighborhood," he said.

"Ah, no, I don't live here."

"Did you say you wanted a sandwich, Miss….." Her sentence trailed off as they seemed to almost lean into me, waiting for my response. It was unnerving and I began to sweat. Keep it together, Jennifer.

"Callahan. Jennifer Callahan. And yes, a sandwich would be nice, thank you."

The man's expression changed to one of surprise as his eyebrows rose into his forehead. The woman walked behind the deli counter.

"What can I make for you, dear?"

"I'm not sure…what do you recommend?"

"The Cobb Club Sandwich is a favorite."

"That sounds great. I'll have that, thank you."

The woman nodded and went to work on making my sandwich. She took out some bread and dressing. The man disappeared back behind the door again.

"So…do you own this place?"

Without stopping her work she smiled. "Yes, my husband Manny and I do. I'm Gloria."

Manny…the man from the file. "Nice to meet you."

"So you said you heard this was a good place for a sandwich. May I ask who recommended us? It's nice to know that our little place has a fan."

Oh shit, I said that, didn't I? "Um, my father did actually. He does business in Los Angeles sometimes." I felt my face get warm as I watched her expression, hoping to read what she was thinking. She remained indifferent as she finished making my sandwich. Maybe she didn't know who my father was and I was just completely overreacting. I watched as she neatly wrapped my sandwich in white parchment paper and placed it in a bag.

"Here you are. Would you like something to drink?"

"Oh, yes. I'll just grab water."

"Okay, I'll meet you up front at the register."

I dug through my wallet and realized I didn't have any cash left so I used my Amex business card. After I finished paying Gloria said, "Thank you Miss Callahan. And please, thank your father for his kind recommendation. Come back again and see us."

"Thank you Gloria, I will."

I picked up my food and walked to the door. I did a double take at the wall at the front. There were photos all hanging neatly in rows. I walked over to take a look.

"That's our wall of fame," Gloria said, coming up behind me.

I scanned the photos of customers, some standing with Manny, some with Gloria. It was then that I saw my father, standing in the middle with one arm around Manny and the other around a young woman who looked strangely familiar to me.

Gloria pointed to the picture. "That's my husband and our daughter, Gabriella, along with a good friend of ours."

"So…you know my father?"

She gaped at me in surprise but quickly recovered. "Oh, I didn't realize…of course…he's like famiglia around here. He saved us and brought our Gabriella here to Manny and me."

Saved them? What the hell…Her reaction struck me as odd. She was being so calm and talking as if she and I were old friends. I was confused.

"We wondered when you would come to ask about Gabriella." She began wringing her hands nervously.

"What about her?"

"Well…she isn't legally here with us. I thought maybe you were here on your father's behalf…"

"Why would I be here for my father, that doesn't make any sense?"

"My husband and I were never able to have children of our own. Your father…when he would come into town he would stop in and say hello…we all became friends. He spoke of you and we admired his love for his family. One day he brought us Gabriella…told us to keep her safe"

"Safe from what?"

"We never asked. We were just so thrilled to finally have a child. He told us the less we knew the better."

"Does he come here often?"

"Just every now and then. I don't know what we were so worried about. Phillip has always been so kind and generous. He's such a wonderful man."

Yeah, Mister Wonderful alright.

"So...you aren't here to talk about Gabriella then?"

It was odd that my father would bring them a child and tell them to keep her safe. None of it made sense and I was worried I had just put a bullseye on my back and these nice people in danger.

"I'm just in town visiting a friend. Please, you have nothing to worry about," I said with my best fake smile. I had to get out of there.

I decided to sit outside at one of the small metal tables so I could think. Gloria's story explained the file about Manny at the beach house, but I just couldn't comprehend the fact that my father had done such an incredible thing for a couple he hardly knew. Or maybe he did know them well, how would I know? Where did my father get a baby to give to these people? The fact that he did someone a favor definitely didn't explain why he went to California all the time. Although that was new information, it hadn't gotten me anywhere with helping Lucas.

After I ate I realized how tired I was, plus I had no idea where I was. I had to get a cab back to the airport and get a hotel room for the night. I decided I would begin to walk back in the direction the cab had brought me, but then stopped, wondering if that was a good idea. Could you even hail a cab here? Maybe I should go back into the deli and ask Gloria for a phonebook. As I tried to figure out what to do, a shiny black limo pulled up to the curb in front of me. The window buzzed down. "Ms. Callahan?"

My mouth dropped open and my heart jumped into my throat. The door opened and the man got out.

"I don't mean to alarm you. My name is Thomas Hawthorne. I'm an associate of your fathers. I was hoping we could talk."

Holy shit. What the hell was going on? Okay, get yourself together Jennifer. I gave myself a mental slap in the face and composed myself. "Associate of my father's? That's a little odd. And how, exactly, did you even know I was here?" I could feel the beads of sweat beginning to form on my forehead as I waited for him to answer.

"Your father called me...said you might be at this store."

"And?" I asked, shifting my weight from one foot to the other. My stomach was getting ready to get rid of my lunch.

"And...your father and I do business together. Phillip mentioned

having a daughter but he failed to mention just how beautiful she was."
He grinned.

I folded my arms, his demeanor making me uncomfortable. "Just what kind of business do you and my father have together?" I asked, ignoring his presumptuous comment. "And why would my father need to call you just because I came here for a sandwich?"

"Yes, I suppose it is a bit theatrical of me to show up like this. I apologize. I was just hoping I would catch you before you left is all. Why don't we go back to my office and we can talk. You obviously have a lot of questions and I'm happy to answer them. Let's get off the street, shall we?"

He kept evading my question. The guy must be out of his mind. What kind of a person just showed up and thought he could whisk me to his office and I'd comply without question? What could he possibly want to talk to me about?

"I don't think so, Mr. Hawthorne. If there's something you think you need to talk to me about, I'll be in town until tomorrow. Maybe we can meet then."

"Please call me Thomas. And if you'd feel more comfortable, maybe we could just talk over dinner?"

"I don't think that's such a good idea," I said. My father knew where I was and for all I knew he had sent Thomas to check up on me. I wasn't ready to trust him completely.

"Which hotel are you staying at?"

"I don't know exactly." I could feel my cheeks flush with embarrassment.

"I'll make you a deal. I know the owner of the Westgate Hotel. I'll make a phone call and arrange a room for you. Once you're settled we can have dinner and talk."

"No, that isn't necessary."

"Please, it would be my pleasure. Plus the owner owes me a favor. Why don't I have the hotel have dinner ready and we can just eat there… if that's okay with you?"

I didn't answer him right away because I didn't want to seem desperate. But I was. I was desperate to help Lucas. And just like floodgates opening I realized what an incredible opportunity it could be. But there was no way I was getting in his car with him.

"Alright then, just a quick dinner and that's it. I have an early flight tomorrow and I would really just like to get some sleep."

He smiled wickedly and laughed. "What else would there be?"

"I'll meet you at the hotel later." I heard my phone ding telling me I had a text message. I ignored it and went back into the deli to ask Gloria if she could call me a cab.

Chapter Nine

In the cab, I looked at my phone. There were three text messages and two missed calls, all from Lucas. SHIT! I checked the texts.

Just wanted 2 say I missed u.
Didn't hear back from u...everything ok?
I called & u didn't answer. I'm worried!

I had to call him. But what would I say? If I told him I was in California who knew what he would do. "Jennifer...where have you been? I've been so worried! Are you alright?"

"Yes, I'm fine. I'm sorry I worried you. My...phone died. I didn't realize it right away." I squeezed my eyes shut as guilt replaced the blood in my veins. I hated lying to him.

"Shit Jennifer, I was going crazy here. I almost took a flight back to North Carolina."

"I've missed you," I whispered.

I heard him sigh. "I've missed you too Jen. The thoughts of what could have happened to you..." His voice trailed off.

"I'll be home in a couple of days. I plan to hold you to your promise of making me dinner when I get home."

"I don't know if seeing each other is such a good idea. I don't want to risk putting you in any danger."

"No one will see us if we're in my apartment."

"We do have some catching up to do. What time does your flight arrive in New York?"

"3:45. Sam will be at the airport to bring me home so I should be there around 4:30. Will you be there waiting for me?"

There was silence on the other end and I wondered what he was thinking. Was he still there? Finally he spoke. "Okay, you've got yourself a deal. I'll be there with dinner and maybe even a dessert, if you're good."

I hugged myself in delight. I couldn't wait to get home. "I'll be good...I promise."

"So what have you been doing since I left?"

Oh shit, why did he have to ask me that? "Oh you know, just reading." That wasn't technically a lie. I'd been reading all those files from the closet.

"Okay, well I won't keep you anymore. Now that I know you're alright I'll let you get back to your reading. Don't worry me like that again, okay?"

My heart melted into a puddle, guilt mixed with devotion. "I'm sorry." For a lot of things that I can't tell you about.

"Have a good night."

"You too. Bye."

"Bye."

A few minutes later the cab pulled up at the front doors to the lobby of the hotel. I paid and got out, going straight to the reception desk to check in.

"Good evening, may I help you?"

"Good evening. Ah, I'm Jennifer Callahan…I believe there should be a room reserved?"

"Yes, we have the room all ready and dinner will be brought up as soon as you're ready." She slid two key cards across the desk to me.

"Thank you."

"We hope you enjoy your stay."

The room was elegant; decorated in golds and corals with a lavish view of the city from the balcony. There was a knock at the door.

"Yes?"

"It's Thomas."

Jesus, did he follow me? "Just a minute."

I opened the door to see Thomas smiling smugly.

"Hey, come in."

"Thank you. Are you getting settled in alright?"

"Well, I just got here actually. And this room is way too much. This is incredibly unnecessary."

"Nonsense, I told you, the owner owes me a favor."

"Well, I'm sorry you had to cash your favor in on me. You won't get to enjoy any of the rewards."

"I feel like I'm benefiting just fine Ms. Callahan. And my reward is yet to come."

Oh shit, he's flirting with me. "Call me Jennifer, and I wouldn't get too ahead of yourself, Thomas. I agreed to have dinner and a conversation with you, that's it. When we're finished I'm kicking you out."

He didn't say anything but seemed surprised.

"I'm sorry to be so stand-offish with you Thomas. I'm just not used to men showing up in limos and then having dinner with them." I tried to remain calm even though that was far from how I felt.

"I'm sorry too. We didn't start out on the right foot, did we? I don't normally do things like this afternoon. I was just trying to help out your father. The last thing I expected was to find a beautiful woman with the attitude of a mountain lion. Why don't we start over?"

I looked at him, confused. "Start over...how, exactly?"

A devilish smile appeared on his face. Oh shit, what was he thinking?

"Why don't we go out some place for dinner tonight?"

"No I don't think so Thomas. I don't have clothes with me to go out. Please, you don't have to go all out to impress me or anything. Let's just keep this simple for now and just have dinner here, okay?"

"As you wish. But I'd like to take you out one day and do just that... impress you."

His eyes were gleaming and I had to fight the urge to jump off the balcony. I felt my face flush and I turned around, hoping he wouldn't notice. This felt wrong, so wrong. My stomach ached as I thought about Lucas and how furious he would be with me for everything that had happened; especially if he found out that I was with an attractive, strange man and was about to have dinner with him. He had warned me I might not be safe, but I pushed my fear back and reminded myself I was there to help Lucas.

Thomas took off his suit jacket and hung it on the chair at the desk. His shoulders were broad and I could see his biceps flex through his shirt. He clearly worked out. "Are you ready to eat now?"

"Yes, thank you."

So far things seemed to be going smoothly. After speaking with room service, he sat down. I sat on the edge of the bed and kicked off my shoes.

"So does your father know why you're here?" he asked.

Shit, my father. "I don't have to ask my father for permission to do things. I haven't done that in quite a long time. What I don't seem to understand is why he felt the need to call you?"

He started laughing. "There's that mountain lion again. I thought I was taming her a bit but I guess not. Your father raves about his shark of a daughter who takes no prisoners in the court room."

That was surprising. "While that may be true, you didn't answer my question."

"As I said before, he was worried that perhaps you were lost. Your father is a good man and a shrewd businessman, that's for sure."

"You said you were an associate of my father's. What does that mean exactly?"

There was a knock at the door and Thomas raised his eyes to the ceiling as if relieved. "I'll get it." He opened the door and a young man wheeled a cart into the room.

"Will there be anything else?" the man asked, looking at both me and Thomas.

"No, thank you," Thomas replied as he handed him a folded bill of money.

The young man left and Thomas wheeled the cart all the way to the table against the windows.

"Shall we eat?"

I stood up, eyeing him suspiciously. Don't think you're off the hook from my question.

"I hope you like what I chose," he said, sitting down.

I removed the silver lid slowly and saw veal tenderloin, potato gnocchi, cauliflower, and mushrooms. It smelled delicious and my stomach began to growl.

"You approve?"

"Yes, this looks good." I said. He poured me a glass of wine. It was dry and bitter...not my favorite but I drank it anyway. I placed my napkin in my lap. "So...you don't just play golf occasionally with my father, do you?"

He leaned back in his chair while chewing, holding his wine. He slowly took a sip and placed the glass back on the table. "No, you're right; I don't just have a causal friendship with Philip."

I put down my fork and folded my arms, trying my best to be patient because his evasiveness was really pissing me off. I had had enough of all the cryptic shit that had been going on all day.

Thomas sighed. "Philip and I met while I was still practicing law. After I accepted a job here he became a consultant for me."

"What kind of consultant?"

"He takes care of all the legal things."

"Why can't you do that if you're a lawyer?"

"I run a very large shipping business here."

"Shipping business?" I asked, remembering the files from the beach house.

"Yes, I'm responsible for a lot of goods that come through these waters. Your father and I play golf whenever he's in town. He talks a great deal about you. He's very proud of you."

I found it hard to believe that my father talked about me to anyone. My heart started pounding in my chest. I resented that my father said things to people that he never said to me, especially to a guy like this. I couldn't help but feel betrayed that he kept me at such arm's length.

"Do you know anything about the shipping business, Jennifer?"

"Not a whole lot, but what does that matter?"

"Because I have my hands full with the responsibilities of running a complex business. I don't have time to be a lawyer too. Your father helps me out a great deal."

We continued to eat our dinner in silence as I thought about Thomas's explanation. I supposed it did make sense and my father didn't have to tell me everything he did. Maybe if I asked he would tell me, who knew. I didn't think I'd ever given him the chance; I'd been so focused on being pissed at him all the time.

My head was reeling from pure fatigue compounded with jet lag. I had to get this Lothario out of my hotel room so I could get a grip on all the events of the day.

Pushing my plate back I wiped my mouth. "Well, that was delicious. Thank you again for the meal and the room."

"You're most welcome. It was my pleasure. I only wish we could have met under different circumstances. We could have gotten to know each other a whole lot better." I had to get him out.

"Well, if you don't mind I'd really like to get some sleep now. I have such an early flight tomorrow."

Without argument he retrieved his jacket from the back of the chair and took his time putting it on, fiddling with his collar and sleeves. Let's go already!

"You know, I have business in New York next week. I would really love to take you out to dinner while I'm there."

Oh holy hell, this guy wouldn't quit.

"Here's my business card. Think about it and call me."

He held out the card to me and I accepted it reluctantly. I looked at it briefly and then did a double take. It read 'Thomas Hawthorne COO, Wallace Industries.' Wallace Industries? As in Vance Wallace Industries? Holy shit. This guy was connected to Vance Wallace too. I had to find out how.

"I'll think about it Thomas. I have your card now so we'll stay in touch."

Chapter Ten

Thomas closed the door lightly as he left and I sighed heavily. At last I was alone. I felt dirty. From the long day? From my behavior? Whatever it was, I was sure a shower to scrub off Thomas's sleaze was the only thing that would make me feel better. I went into the lavish bathroom with its plush floor mats and giant floral arrangement between the double sinks. I had to turn three knobs to turn the shower on and it wasn't long until the room was filled with steam. I removed my clothes and just left them in a heap on the floor, anxious to get in.

I had brought a hard loofah scrubber in with me from the basket of goodies on the counter. I squirted some soap on it and washed myself thoroughly. It felt good as the hot water cascaded down me, removing all the day's stress and tension. It didn't, however, take any of the uncertainty away. As I washed my hair I ran through the day's events in my head. The way Manny had behaved; so stand offish and nervous. Why had my father done such a favor for another man? And Thomas…he was certainly a piece of work. A mixture of sleaze and charm wrapped up in a catalog model smile. If he didn't have time to be a lawyer when it came to the shipping business then how did he have time to schmooze me?

As I finished rinsing my hair I decided I no longer wanted to try to figure everything out right then. What I had to do was get everything out of my head and down on paper while it was still fresh. I rinsed off and got out of the shower. I tied my hair up in one towel and wrapped another around my wet, naked body and went out to my overnight bag. I pulled out the file that I had made and sat on the bed. I scribbled down everything I could think of that would be relevant: Manny and daughter, favor from dad, Thomas Hawthorne, shipping business for Vance Wallace. I finished and put it aside, lying back on the pillows.

I wondered what Lucas was doing right then. He would be furious with me for being in California. What he didn't know wouldn't hurt him for now. So far all that had happened had been fairly harmless, with the exception of the way Thomas was behaving with me. If I could just manage some phony feelings for a while and maybe get a little more information out of him, then I could let him down easy; tell him things wouldn't work out and leave it at that. No harm, no foul. And in the process I could help Lucas.

అంళ

The next day I was almost two hours early for my flight back to Virginia. I decided to have some coffee and eat while I waited. I found a Starbucks and took my seat in front by the window, reading the paper and eating an egg and cheese croissant. As I turned the page of the paper I noticed a man sitting in one of the empty terminal waiting areas. He was wearing black pants and a navy golf shirt, and a pair of black sunglasses. He reminded me of the guy Lucas and I had seen when we were running on Memorial Day. It couldn't be. I shrugged it off and finished my coffee.

The flight was uneventful and quick. As I left the plane and was walking through the airport towards the parking lot, I noticed the man from the airport back in California. He was walking in the same direction I was, but on the other side of the hallway, and I couldn't help but feel as though something wasn't quite right. It could easily just have been coincidence that we had been on the same flight, both of us walking to cars in the parking lot, although I hadn't seen him on the plane, nor was he carrying any luggage. I wasn't convinced of the coincidence scenario and decided he was creepy and my gut knew better. I saw a ladies room coming up ahead and ducked inside. There were a few women at sinks and one stall door was closed. I wasn't sure what to do so I just went into a stall. After what felt like an eternity and wondering if that was long enough, I decided to see if I could finish the trek to my rental car.

I looked down both ends of the hallway and saw no sign of Mr. Creepy. Of course I knew that didn't mean he was gone and he could very well be out in the parking lot; a place where there were less people around and nowhere for me to hide from him again. Maybe I should have a security guard walk me to my car? I considered that briefly until I got to the doors outside and saw it was broad daylight and there were several people waiting at the stop for the parking lot tram. I walked quickly over and waited anxiously until the tram arrived and I was safely on board, no Mr. Creepy in sight. I was being completely paranoid. I rolled my eyes at myself and relaxed a bit.

∂◦◦

I arrived back at the beach house just after six and I was starving. I dropped my bag at the door and went straight to the kitchen. I opened the fridge and saw the things that Lucas had bought at the store the night he showed up unexpectedly; the night I had finally confessed to him all that I knew about his past. My heart felt heavy remembering that but my stomach overruled my sadness and called for a salami sandwich. I slapped it together and wolfed it down together with a bunch of grapes that were just past their prime. I went into the living room to sit down. Oh shit...all those stupid files were still there. I stepped over the mess and pulled out my phone. I was feeling incredibly homesick so I called Lucas.

"Hey, is everything okay?" he asked.

"Hello to you too," I said with a laugh. "Yeah everything's fine. I'm bored and homesick so I've decided maybe I'll come home a day early." I flopped down on the couch and pulled my feet up behind me.

"Well, that's definitely good news. I would love to have you back in the city where I can keep an eye on you and know you're safe."

"Will you still be at my apartment when I get there?"

"Of course, I've been looking forward to it. Do you have your new flight info yet?"

"No, not yet. I wanted to call you first."

"Well I'm glad you did. Now hurry up and change the flight and text me when you have it."

"I can't wait to see you."

"Me too. I'll talk to you soon."

I looked out the window, twirling my favorite strand of hair. Why hadn't I just fallen for a man who didn't have so much shit going on in his life that also involved my father? It would make for a great soap opera. That kind of drama didn't happen to regular people.

I decided to get up and clean up the mess, and then I got my computer out and changed my flight plans. I called Sam and let him know that I would be back a day early and he happily agreed to meet me at the airport.

I packed the rest of my belongings and emptied the fridge of what little food was in there. I found a bottle of red wine that Lucas had also gotten from the store and decided to treat myself. I poured myself a glass and took it and the bottle to the bedroom and texted Lucas.

All set for tomorrow. I should be home around 7:30 in the evening. What's for dinner?

I took a big sip of wine. It was sweet and delicious. I propped up some pillows and leaned back as I took another big sip. I heard my phone.

Me. ;)

Oh, I loved it when he flirted with me! I giggled at his response and hugged my knees, grinning. Oh, the dirty things I wanted to write back to him....but I didn't. I knew Lucas was adamant about keeping our contact to a minimum. I settled for a simple response and left it at that.

Sounds yummy...can't wait. Good night!

≈∞≈

Just as I was getting settled in my seat on the plane my phone began to ring and I thought for sure it was Lucas. I looked at the caller ID - my father. Holy shit...what the hell was he calling me for? Knowing I would have the excuse of having to turn my phone off soon I answered.

"Hello Daddy, how are you?"

"Hello Jennifer. I was just calling to see how things were going."

Everything in my gut was telling me it wasn't just a social call. He had known that I had been in California and I was sure he had spoken to Thomas. What the hell had Thomas told my father? I went with a playing dumb tactic.

"Actually I got bored and am about to fly out of Virginia right now to come home. I guess it's just too quiet for me...not like the city that's for sure." Oh my gosh, I was the worst liar. I shook my head a little hoping he didn't pick up on it.

"Oh...well I'm sorry things didn't go as you had planned. I forgot to mention that there were some of your mother's things stored there."

My heart started pounding. Holy fuck. "Really, what things?"

"Oh just some old keepsakes of hers. They were in a closet, you didn't see them?"

"No I didn't, but I wish I had."

"Maybe next time then. I'll make sure to send the cleaning service out tomorrow."

Cleaning service? He was worried about having the house cleaned? Or was he going to send someone to check on the files?

86

"I'll have to go there more often and get reacquainted with the area. It was lonely being there all by myself."

"Yes, I can imagine it was. Your mother loved it there and took you every chance she got." His voice sounded low and sad. I hated talking to him about my mother. Thankfully the announcement came over the intercom telling the passengers to turn off electronics and to fasten seatbelts.

"I have to go now Daddy...we're about to take off."

"Yes, well, have a safe flight and I'll see you at the office next week then."

"OK...goodbye."

"Goodbye Jennifer."

My heart sank down into my stomach as I watched the world get smaller as the plane flew into the clouds. He hadn't said a word about me being in California.

かの

A half hour later I walked outside to see Sam waiting for me at the curb. He was a welcome sight after a stressful week of what was supposed to have been a vacation for me. I chuckled at the irony.

"Hello Ms. Callahan, how was your trip?"

"It was kind of boring actually, thank you Sam."

As we drove away, Sam turned to look at someone walking past. Just as we turned a corner, I managed to catch a glimpse - it was the man from the airport. No way, it couldn't have been.

"So how was your week here, Sam? What did you do while I was gone?"

Our eyes met in the rear view mirror and I could tell he was stalling.

"Um...well, I drove your father a few times to meetings, but that's about it really."

Hmmm...why would Sam be weird about driving my father? I wondered if he was trying to tell me something without actually telling me but my phone interrupted my thoughts.

Hey...ready and waiting. C u soon.

My heart rate kicked up a notch as I thought of Lucas at my apartment. I wondered what he was doing. Was he actually cooking something? The little girl in me was bouncing up and down in the seat clapping her hands as the excitement grew. I felt my face getting hot, no doubt from my increasing rise in blood pressure. The devil in me was sitting back, legs crossed and smoking a cigarette, fanning herself seductively.

As Sam pulled off into Manhattan there was lingering rush hour traffic and I cursed every red light. Finally we arrived at my apartment and I practically burst out of the car.

"Would you like me to help you take your bags upstairs?" Sam asked.

"No! I mean, that's okay, Sam. You go home, I've got it."

He smiled and gave me a wink. "Have a good night."

My heart was pounding out of my chest as the anticipation of seeing Lucas grew. I took a deep breath trying to calm myself down. I opened the door - the room was dimly lit with candles everywhere. I heard soft piano music coming from the stereo and the room smelled like lavender...my favorite. Lucas was in the doorway to the kitchen and I was entranced. He was wearing jeans with a button-up shirt that hung un-tucked, the top two buttons undone. He was leaning against the door frame with his left hand in the pocket of his jeans. The dim light cast half his face in shadow making his eyes seem dark and devilish. He had a slight grin on his face as we stared, green eyes locked to blue. It had been so long since I had been with a man intimately I wasn't sure if I would know what to do and a wave of nervousness washed over me.

My emotions took over and I was no longer able to curb the appetite I had tried hard to suppress for so long. The sight of him, the look on his face, his strong body practically holding up the wall, even the smell of the lavender...it was all that I had run here for. I dropped my bags and walked purposefully toward him. He took his hand from his pocket, almost like he knew he was going to need to brace himself.

Our eyes never left each other and we collided into a passionate kiss. We were all hands and kisses and panting and lust. I wanted him right then, right there. I fumbled with frustration as I unbuttoned his shirt with shaky hands. He put his hands over mine and our eye met. My posture softened as I looked at him. I smiled shyly like a teenager, scared and unsure if it was okay. He smiled back at me and the nervousness melted away. I finally reached the last button and took a moment to admire his strong, muscular body. I pushed his shirt off and ran my hands slowly down his sculpted body to the button of his jeans. He grabbed at the hem of my shirt and pulled it over my head. Then he unbuttoned my jeans. We both kicked off our shoes and quickly undressed. Before I knew it, he had me up against the wall. He lifted me with ease and I wrapped my legs around his waist. Holy shit, this was awkward! I felt him push into me and I no longer cared about awkward. I moaned into his neck, delightfully accepting the feeling.

I felt his lips brush against my ear. "Well worth the wait."

I moaned again at the sound of his voice and put my head back up against the wall as he thrusted into me over and over. He stopped and, still inside me, carried me to the bed, laying down over me. With his elbows on either side of my head he was able to look right at me. We were moving in such a perfect rhythm I became overwhelmed with desire. He must have seen the look on my face because he picked up his pace until I cried out with an orgasm but even then he didn't stop. I wrapped my legs tightly around him, never wanting the moment to end. He kept going and going until I came again. He finished with me that time and I was left panting and sweaty beneath his strong body, trembling with aftershock, clinging to him with my arms and legs.

He lay down next to me and our breathing slowed as we settled down. I curled up in his arms, caressing his skin in the afterglow. I felt his hand find mine and we entwined our fingers together. For the first time since he had left the beach house I was happy and relaxed. For now.

Chapter Eleven

I could still hear the music playing from the living room and it was darker now. The evening was turning into night so I switched on a lamp on the nightstand. I rolled over onto my side and leaned my head in my hand. Lucas had his eyes closed but I could tell he was awake by the slight smile on his face. I traced every feature of his face with my eyes, memorizing them. It felt like months since I'd seen him and I wanted to soak in of every inch of him. His chin had a dusting of stubble and I could see the creases at the corners of his eyes more clearly. His hair was no longer in place since my hands had invaded every strand during our reunion.

"Well, we seem to have indulged in having our dessert first," I said softly. With his eyes still closed his grin grew wider. "I don't know about you, but I'm starved."

He rolled over and mirrored how I was laying, putting his head in his hand. He leaned in and gently kissed my lips.

"I'm definitely hungry. Something came up earlier," he said pushing my hair back behind my shoulder, not meeting my eyes. "I wasn't able to get here with enough time to cook. We can order in, though."

Hmm…I wonder what it was that came up. I hated to ruin our magical reunion but I wanted to make sure my being in California hadn't created any kind of trouble here. I sat up to face him and tucked the sheet under my arms.

"Did something happen?"

"No, nothing that you're thinking." He smiled, then stood up and put his jeans back on. "I've been moving all day. I found a place not too far from here."

"What? Why are you moving?"

He laughed lightly. "Take that look off your face please. I'm not a crazy stalker okay?"

I smiled at the way he read me so well. Stalker…technically I was the stalker so that wasn't the word I would choose. Paranoid maybe?

"You don't have to protect me from anything Lucas. I really think you're overreacting about all this. Vance Wallace probably doesn't even know I exist." I didn't believe that for one second.

"You have no idea how much Wallace knows and I wouldn't put anything past him. You shouldn't either, Jen. This is very serious and I wish you would stop acting like it's no big deal." The crease between his eyes had gotten deeper and his voice was slightly raised. "You know exactly what he's capable of." He closed his eyes as his face filled with anguish and he began rubbing the back of his neck. I knew he was thinking of his parents. I got up and went to him.

"I'm sorry, you're right," I said, burying my head in his chest. He wrapped his arms around me and squeezed me tight.

"I don't want anything to happen to you. I feel much better having you back in the city." He kissed my hair and I felt his concern seep into me. God, I'd missed this man!

"Why don't we go out to eat? There's a place just down the road."

"I don't think that's a good idea Jen. Someone could see us. It's bad enough I'm here now."

I pulled out of his embrace and cradled his face in my hands as he knotted his fingers behind my waist. "I know what you're worried about - and I understand why. But I've finally met someone. I feel excited again. Can't we enjoy it like regular people? There's a pizza place just down the street we can walk to, have a slice and we can come right back when we're done." I smiled lightly and batted my eyes knowing I was probably trying his patience. I wanted so badly to spend time with him like a regular couple.

He closed his eyes and breathed in softly, letting it out with a sigh. "Fine, you win. But just a slice and we're coming right home, agreed?"

"Agreed." I kept my expression flat but inside I was doing cartwheels.

I quickly got dressed in jeans and a t-shirt, pulled my hair into a pony tail and we were off. Once we were outside Lucas put his arm around my shoulder and pulled me close while his eyes darted all over the place. His embrace wasn't that of a carefree-let's-walk-down-the-street kind of way. It was more protective, which made me nervous so I began looking all over the place too. There really wasn't much going on since it was late there weren't many people around.

The air outside was warm with a cool breeze blowing. It was such a nice night out and I was glad Lucas had agreed to leave the apartment. I'd been cooped up in airplanes and hotel rooms for too long. I needed a night out. I put my arm around Lucas's waist and gave him a soft squeeze. He looked down at me with his mouth pressed into a thin line, eyebrows knitted together.

"Hey, lighten up, okay?" I said with a smile.

His face softened briefly as he gave me a fake smile but then he turned back to his business of scanning our surroundings. I gave up the battle of trying to get him to relax; I mean, who was I kidding? He was a cop and would behave that way by nature anyway. But the fact that his demeanor was so tight and serious was making me resentful when all I wanted was a normal night with my new boyfriend.

At Antonio's I breathed in the heavenly scent of garlic, tomato sauce and parmesan cheese. I was so hungry and I could hardly wait to eat. The room was dimly lit with small round tables in the center with red and white checkered table cloths. Around the perimeter of the room were booths; Lucas pulled me straight to one in the back and waited while I sat down before he positioned himself so he could get a clear view of the door. There was only one other couple in the place with us so it was quiet, other than the soft music playing.

"Just a slice."

"Okay, okay." I smiled.

"What?"

"Nothing. I just feel safe with you. Thank you for taking such good care of me."

He reached across the table and took my hands. "As much as I hate to admit it, this place seems quiet enough…kind of romantic, actually."

I squeezed his hands and simply replied with a satisfied smile. I wanted to tell him a big fat I told you so but I opted against it.

Our waitress came to the table and we released hands. We each ordered a slice of pizza and sodas, which arrived at our table in no time. We ate quickly; me because I was hungry, Lucas because he was nervous. The waitress came back to our table.

"Can I get you folks anything else?"

"Yes, I'd like another slice please," I said, not feeling at all satisfied.

"No, just a slice remember."

"Fine." I directed a kind smile at the now uncomfortable waitress. "Could I just have that to go please?"

"Of course, I'll be right back."

The waitress disappeared and I glared at Lucas.

"Look, I don't like being out in the open like this. I just want to get back to the apartment."

I gave up the battle of trying to get him to chill out - I was obviously never going to win. After that the atmosphere between us was tense. Lucas was fidgeting with the small jar of parmesan on the table, spinning it and looking at the door every other minute. When the waitress came back with my to-go bag, Lucas paid the bill at the register and we were once again outside, walking back to my apartment. We walked quickly, holding hands and not talking. It wasn't the most romantic date I'd ever been on.

As we approached the front door of my building, I saw a man across the street leaning against a fence. When he saw me notice him he immediately put his head down and walked away. Holy shit, was that guy watching us? I quickly looked to Lucas who obviously hadn't seen the man because he was unlocking the door. He handed me my keys once the door was open and I fumbled with them and dropped them.

"Hey, you okay?" he asked.

"I just saw a guy across the street. I think your paranoia is rubbing off on me." He looked at me hesitantly then looked out to the street and back and forth before meeting my eyes again.

"What did he look like?"

"I don't know…I didn't get a good look. He walked away."

"Come on, let's get inside."

We rode in the elevator in silence. I was mentally waving my hand in the air, telling myself I was reading too much into things. But what if it was someone watching us? Had Lucas been right this whole time?

When we arrived back inside my apartment the smell of lavender still lingered in the air. I dropped my purse on the couch and turned to Lucas, pulling on his hand. "Come on, let's go take a shower."

We lingered in the shower for a while, washing each other. That led to kissing which led to us making love a second time under the running water. After we got out of the shower we dried off and got right into bed. Lucas told me about his new apartment and, since it was only four blocks away from my place, I was secretly hoping we'd get to see each other more often. What better way to be protected than to have a cop sleeping in my bed. Lucas pulled me close with my back against his chest and I snuggled in as if it were the most natural thing in the world. I drifted off to sleep without any worries, but woke startled by the recurring nightmare of my mother and the car crash. I looked around the room frantically as if she were there. That look of anguish she had had as she tried to get to me was imprinted on my brain and I wanted to find her, tell her I was okay. But she was nowhere in sight. I was in my apartment again as the images of the car faded away. It was so real. I felt like I had really been there. But it was just a dream.

I sat up, drenched in sweat. I looked over and saw Lucas wasn't in bed. I pulled on my robe over my damp, sweaty skin and walked out into the living room, to find him standing at a window, looking outside. He was wearing his jeans but was shirtless with his hands tucked into his pockets. He looked ethereal leaning against the window with the soft moon light shining on his face and chest. But the look on his face was anything but angelic; his eyebrows were pushed together and his jaw was clenched. What was he thinking about?

"Lucas?" He turned his head in my direction and his body language changed immediately. His shoulders softened and he turned to face me.

"Hey, what are you doing up?"

"I had a bad dream." He opened his arms to me and I walked directly into them. He was warm and smelled like the soap from the shower. I felt safe with his arms around me, making the memory of my bad dream dissipate.

"You want to talk about it?"

"No, not really. What are you doing up?" I picked my head off of his chest and looked at him, hoping to read his face.

He kissed my forehead and smiled. "I just couldn't sleep." I didn't believe him but my gut was telling me not to press him. "You want some coffee?" he asked.

"Yeah, might as well. What time is it anyway?"

"It's almost six. I guess I'm still on third shift hours."

As I walked over to the sofa to sit down I noticed my bags were still at the door where I had dropped them. I remembered the red folder. While Lucas was in the kitchen making coffee I grabbed my overnight bag and tucked it under the chair to my desk. I still had to figure out a way to tell him about it.

I sat on the sofa and tucked my feet under me. After a few minutes Lucas came in with a cup of coffee, made just the way I liked it with cream and sugar. I accepted with a smile, noticing how good it felt to have someone here to share insomnia with. It was Friday and I still had three more glorious days left before I had to be back at work, which reminded me that Lucas should be starting his new job on Monday too.

"So, are you getting nervous about starting your new job?"

"Nah, it's nothing I haven't done before. I look at it as a way to make money and occupy my time until I get my real job back." His tone was impassive as he got comfortable next to me on the sofa.

Oh, so he planned to be a detective again? "Do you think that's a possibility? I mean, I thought the police shrink said it wasn't an option."

"Yeah, a year ago it wasn't. But I'm starting to remember things… little bits here and there. Pretty soon it will all come back to me and I can move on with life."

Hmm…he seemed pretty confident about that. I couldn't shake the feeling that there was something he wasn't telling me.

"Something happened while I was away, didn't it?" He looked at me and his mouth fell open. Bingo, I'd hit the nail on the head. "Whatever it is you can tell me."

He ran a hand through his messy hair and crossed his ankle over his knee. "I had a visit from your friend Lamb the other day." He took a sip of coffee.

What the hell? I leaned forward and put my coffee down so I could turn to face Lucas better. As I tried to figure out which question to ask first, Lucas reached over and touched my hand, breaking my concentration.

"Don't get all worked up."

I couldn't help but laugh. I felt like I was going a little bit insane with everything that'd been happening lately, plus it wasn't cute just then how well he was reading me. And why was he being so damn calm?

"I'm just trying to understand. What did he want?"

"Well, in a nutshell he was checking up on me and my intentions with you. He asked me how we met, how long we've been seeing each other, he even asked me how serious it was between us. It was kind of father-like, really."

I couldn't believe what I was hearing. I was so pissed at Lamb I wanted to wring his neck. Why the hell was he questioning Lucas about shit that was none of his business? Was he spying on me for my father? Why couldn't Daddy just ask me about any of this?

"So what did you tell him?"

"I didn't tell him anything. I knew right away something was off as soon as I saw him at the door. I didn't trust him one bit and neither should you." His tone became serious.

Not so calm anymore. "I was being evasive with him too. Lamb is a man who likes to find out information and when he doesn't get it from one place he moves on to the next. He was just checking up on me, that's all. He's harmless," I said, rolling my eyes.

"I doubt that."

"What do you mean? What aren't you telling me?"

He hesitated. He began picking imaginary lint off his jeans. It seemed like an eternity before he answered.

"After he finally left I couldn't shake the feeling that something was off but I couldn't put my finger on it. I went to bed that night and had a dream but realized when I woke up it was actually a memory of something."

Oh shit, I didn't know if I wanted to hear any more of this! I chewed on the inside of my cheek as I waited for him to continue.

"I've seen George Lambert before the day he came to my apartment. It was while I was undercover and I regularly hung out at Wallace's office. I watched Wallace clap Lamb on the shoulder like they were old friends and then they shook hands. They had a brief meeting, Wallace handed Lamb a small, overstuffed envelope and Lamb walked right past me as he left."

I stood up and started pacing around the living room. My head was once again swimming. I stopped and looked at Lucas in disbelief.

"No…no way. There's no way that George Lambert works with scum like Vance Wallace. He must have been doing something undercover himself, doing work for a case or something." Yeah, that sounded rational, didn't it? "I know him…he's like a father to me. He must have just been playing a role to get information."

Lucas stood up and took me by the shoulders. "Jennifer, think about it. Your father represents Wallace. Lamb wouldn't have to spy on him."

I backed away from him, shaking my head a little, trying to absorb what he'd said. Reality began to set in. All I had been doing wasn't just about helping Lucas get justice for his parents anymore. It was so much more. Everything I thought was real or true was now all a big lie. And I was smack dab in the middle of it. I wondered how long I had been walking around that law firm thinking I was doing my job and helping people when really I was oblivious to the fact that I worked at a place that didn't follow the law at all.

Who else was in on all this? I started pacing around the room again with my hands on my hips while I ran through every employee in the firm through my mind. My assistant Karen? She could have been keeping tabs on me for my father; telling him about my appointments and schedule. I ran quickly through the few other lawyers, realizing they were automatically on the shit list as far as I was concerned. I didn't know who to trust anymore.

I stopped pacing and looked to Lucas for some kind of clarity to my crazy thoughts; some direction that I could switch to so all of it made sense. Terror started welling up into my chest like a rising flood and it must have been all over my face too, because Lucas came over to me. He wrapped his arms around me and stroked my hair, swaying slowly. I stood statue-like with my hands still at my side. "It's gonna be okay."

I pulled away abruptly. "No, it's not! None of this is okay. I'm hearing all of this and wondering what my father has gotten me into. What am I responsible for, without knowing? Whatever is going on and shit finally hits the fan, I'll be implicated too, just by association!"

"Stop it Jennifer and calm down." His voice was serious. "I know that you're not involved."

"Oh, so that's gonna make everything work out to my benefit… having a cop as a boyfriend? Yeah, that won't look suspicious." There was more sarcasm in my voice than I had intended. "How am I supposed to go back there and pretend like everything is fine and dandy?" I looked at him and fear replaced my anger. I started to cry as thoughts of all the lies overflowed in my mind; lies from my father, lies from Lamb and, worst of all, my lies to Lucas.

Chapter Twelve

I staggered over to the couch and sat down, letting my sadness go. I cried hard sobs as my thermonuclear fit came to an end. As I calmed down I kept thinking about Lamb and the possibility of him going against my father, actually working with Vance Wallace. How could that be? And why...why would he want to work for someone like that? I trusted Lamb, counted on him, believed in him. He was more like a father to me than my real father had ever been. No, he was a good man...he wasn't capable of working with someone like that. Was he? Ugh...I just didn't know.

I was wiped out and tired beyond thinking. I wanted to wake up from the nightmare and go back to my boring life. No, that's not what I wanted either. I looked up at Lucas and he was standing over me nervously, rubbing his forehead. He sat down and pulled me to him which only made me cry again. I leaned my head on his chest, feeling grateful he was there and knew exactly what I needed. His words from the beach house came to mind. Since meeting you I've felt put back together. I had been walking around like a piece of me was missing too until I met Lucas. I didn't want that feeling to change. Suddenly determination jolted through me like a bolt of lightning.

I stood up, wiped my face and smoothed my hair back out of my face. Lucas was looking at me.

"Don't worry; I got it all out of my system."

"Are you okay?"

"Yeah, I'm fine," I said, shrugging a bit. I picked up my cup of coffee and took a big gulp. It was luke-warm but I didn't care, I needed the caffeine.

"I'm sorry about Lamb."

"It's not your fault, there's nothing to apologize for."

"I know how much he means to you. You don't have to pretend like it doesn't bother you."

"I'm not pretending anything." I immediately regretted my tone and closed my eyes, taking a calming breath. "I'm sorry," I whispered. "It was a shock and a lot to take in. You're right."

"I've been thinking a lot about this the last couple of days and have been in close contact with my old partner, MacCabe, at the station. I want him fully informed on everything I know so if anything develops he can act right away."

"What does that mean? You told the police that you had some memory of George Lambert talking to Vance Wallace once? That doesn't prove anything!"

He stood up, and shot me a dirty look. He took a cup from the cupboard and put it on the counter with a loud bang. He poured the coffee and slammed the pot back into the stand then added cream. He came back into the living room and sat down on the couch.

"That was uncalled for…I'm sorry I said that."

"I know you want to defend him Jen, but before you do, all I ask is that you make sure you get all of your facts straight. You of all people should know how to do that."

Touché. "I just find it hard to believe that what you remember is actually Lamb accepting money for some job he may have done for Wallace. That might be what you think, but to me that just doesn't make any sense."

"No, you're right; I don't know for sure what he was doing there - which is why I want the detectives who are on the case to know any information I may have, right or wrong, and investigate it. I can't help but wonder if he's responsible for my cover being blown."

"I don't want to talk about this anymore. I have this weekend left to enjoy before I have to face reality again Can we please just forget about things for now?"

"I'm getting really pissed about how you seem to just push everything under a rug like it doesn't even exist. What's going on is serious and I wish you would take it that way."

I sat back down next to him. He was right. "I don't know what else to do," I said sadly. "If I admit all of this is real then I'll have to deal with it. And I have no idea how. I don't have a plan. And I hate feeling so vulnerable."

"We will have a plan. But the sooner you face this the quicker we can make one. I moved closer to you because I want to keep a better eye on you. But that's not the only reason. I love you Jennifer. I can't picture my life without you."

Wait, what had he just said? My eyes met his and I realized I really had heard what I thought I'd heard. Although I was surprised to hear him say it, I knew he meant it. I had felt it a hundred times. My heart filled with love and even a trace of hope for the first time in a long time. "I love you too. I feel exactly the same way you do." I leaned into him. I fought the urge to cry again and a lump formed in my throat.

I sat back in my own space and my shoulders slumped. "I just can't stand how hard something so simple has to be. Why does it have to be the firm I work for that is involved with Vance Wallace?"

"We'll figure this all out and have the answers eventually. Right now it's important we stick to a few simple things."

Oh shit. He stood up and started pacing in front of me.

"First, we need to stay away from each other. I'll still stay in close communication with you as best as I can, but we absolutely can't be seen together. Got it?"

"Yeah, I got it." I didn't like the plan already.

"I would appreciate it if you wouldn't roll your eyes." He paused. "Next, if something new comes to light, I want to know about it right away, deal? I want to make sure all information goes straight to Mac at the station so he can make a tight, solid case. I don't want anything slipping through the cracks like last time and Wallace getting away again."

Double shit. I looked over to the bag I had under the chair at my desk. How was I going to tell him about that file? I just had to tell him and get it over with!

"Lastly, if there's an emergency we need to come up with a code, or something only you and I know about."

"What do you mean, an emergency?"

"I mean, if you're in a situation where you don't feel safe and you want help. I want you to call me or text me, let me know somehow that you need me."

I tried hiding an amorous smile.

"What?" he asked.

I couldn't help but feel giddy at the notion of needing Lucas. It felt good all over. "I like it that you want to take care of me."

A look of surprise washed over his face as he stopped his pacing mid-stride. I got up and walked over to him and put my arms around his neck while looking into his eyes. Our gaze locked for a moment and I leaned in and kissed his neck several times.

"Mmm…" He pulled me back and smiled. "Last time before I have to go," he whispered, pulling me into the bedroom.

❧

An hour later Lucas and I were going over some last minute details.

"Okay, so I'll call your cell phone at 7:30 Monday night, got it?"

I walked over to him and knitted my fingers around his waist. "Couldn't you just come over and check on me?"

He laughed lightly and hugged me tight. After a moment he pulled away and took me by the shoulders. "As much as I would love to do that you know I can't. And if there's trouble just text the word 'diner' and I'll track you from there. So it's very important; if your regular routine changes in any way you have to let me know."

He sighed heavily and ran a hand nervously through his hair. He looked around the room as if he was trying to remember something. I reached up and touched his cheek.

"Hey, don't worry, I'll be fine. We've been over all the plans a hundred times…I've got it, I promise."

"Okay, then," He pulled me into a tight embrace and kissed my hair. "I love you. I'll talk to you Monday."

"I love you too."

We separated and I opened the door for him. His shoulders slumped. "Lock every lock," he said with a finger pointing to my door.

"Yes sir."

We shared a laugh but I didn't relish the thought of being alone. I closed the door, locked the chain and the dead bolt then lastly the lock on the doorknob. A wave of sadness washed over me as I remembered how far away Monday was, when I would talk to Lucas again. It felt like we had gotten to that point in a new relationship where we wanted to spend all our time with each other. But instead, we had made plans to avoid each other and only talk if there was an emergency. I shrugged the feeling off and grabbed my bags before heading back to my room. I decided to unpack and check my email, hoping that would keep my mind off of everything for a while.

I changed into some jeans and a t-shirt and switched on some music. I made my bed and unpacked my bags, leaving the red file lying on the foot bench at the end of my bed. As I was picking things up around my room I found Lucas's keys on the floor. Oh shit...he's gonna need these. I should probably call him. But the devil in me came up with a better idea. Once he realized he didn't have them, he'd have to call, or better yet come back. No harm in pretending like I hadn't noticed them. So I put the keys on my night stand and shimmied around the room to the music, feeling proud of myself for my little plan.

After putting all of my suitcases away I sat in the living room with my laptop and brought up my emails. I had thirteen new messages and figured that would keep me occupied for a while. I scanned through the new messages and one in particular caught my eye. It was from Thomas Hawthorne and was dated two nights ago; the night we had had dinner in my hotel room. Holy shit, how did he get my email address?

From: Thomas Hawthorne
Subject: Future meeting
Date: June 18 2012 11:47
To: Jennifer Callahan

Dear Jennifer,

I enjoyed getting to know you at our dinner tonight. I look forward to seeing you again and getting to know you further. As I already told you, I will be in the New York area in a few days so I will be in touch with you. Until then, I hope you enjoy the rest of your stay in California.

Sincerely,
Thomas Hawthorne
COO Wallace Industries

My stomach dropped. I'd been anything but honest with Lucas. That file I had was something he could take to the detectives. And now I was going to have to find a way to deal with Thomas too when he called. Great.

I heard a knock at the door. So Lucas decided to skip calling me and just came back over. I liked the way he thought. I closed my laptop and thought maybe I could make us lunch - I thought I might have some pasta. I unlocked all the locks on my door. As I opened it my smile fell along with my jaw, my heart and lastly my stomach.

"Well that's not the kind of greeting I would've expected from you." I stood there in a daze as worry and confusion washed over me. Oh shit. "I hope you don't mind…I was in the area and wanted to see how your trip went." I still didn't move. "Well? Are you going to invite me in?"

I shook my head a little trying to get my thoughts together. "Of course, come in," I said stepping out of the way. "Can I get you something to drink…coffee?"

"Yeah sure."

I went into the kitchen and stood at the sink while I rinsed and filled the coffee pot. I heard him behind me as he shuffled into the room and my stomach jumped into my throat. "So how did you know I was home?" My whole body stiffened when I heard my voice crack. I was sure he could tell how tense I was.

"When were you going to tell me that Lucas Benjamin was your boyfriend?" He asked the question so calmly and coolly, completely ignoring my question. "You've really disappointed me the past couple of days, you know that?"

What the hell? How did he know about Lucas? I looked over my shoulder to see if I could read his expression. I was wondering, hoping even, that he was testing me to see what I would say. But he was just standing there with his arms folded. Past couple of days? I looked back to the sink and it hit me. Oh my God, the man at the airport…the man on the street. There was someone watching me! I felt like such a fool for not telling Lucas.

"What makes you think I have anything going on with Lucas Benjamin?"

"Don't cross examine me - I'm not some insignificant schmuck."

Okay, plan B. "What business is it of yours anyway who I do and do not know?"

I heard him chuckle softly. "You know what? You're right, that is none of my business. But you being in California and falsely representing yourself, is."

Oh shit. The inquisition was over and my gut was telling me I had to get out of there, but I wasn't sure how. My mind was racing with a thousand thoughts. I was scared because now I didn't know what he was capable of. Where's Lucas? What was that stupid code word? Beach…

no...limo...no...oh God what was it? I was so nervous I couldn't think straight. Why hasn't he come back yet? I heard someone else come into the room and looked over my shoulder. I didn't recognize the man but I knew something bad was about to happen.

I looked down at the now full coffee pot and slowly turned the water off. I tightened my grip around the handle as my instincts to protect myself started to kick in. I hesitated though. Would he hurt me? I heard my cell ring and I turned towards the sound. Something hit me in the back of the head. I dropped the coffee pot and heard it shatter as I landed on my side, hitting my hip and shoulder hard against the wood floor. "Ohhh..." I moaned. I reached up and touched my head where a hot searing pain was throbbing. I felt the warmth of my own blood on my fingers and bile filled my throat. I tried to push myself up but I put my arm on a piece of the glass from the coffee pot, and the pain made me slump back down again. I was dizzy and disoriented but I knew I had to get up.

"You don't have to do this." I groaned. "You don't understand...."

"Why the hell did you have to hit her, you asshole? Everything was perfect and now you've ruined it." I had never heard him so angry before.

My mind was swimming. Why was he doing this What was going to happen? Where was Lucas? I had to call Lucas. I looked at him, blinking several times trying to focus. I could see his distorted image kneeling over me and then felt him put something over my mouth and nose. I tried with every last ounce of energy I could muster to get away, but it was futile - everything went black.

Chapter Thirteen

I heard muted voices and I wondered who was in my apartment. I opened my eyes and immediately had to close them again - the light was piercing my brain. My head felt like it was two sizes too big for my body and it hurt...bad. I wanted to touch the back where one spot seemed to be throbbing the most but, when I tried to move, my arm wouldn't budge. And neither would the other one.

I opened my eyes a little, allowing them to adjust to the light. As the room came into focus, I looked around. This wasn't my apartment. There were huge floor to ceiling windows on the wall to my left. In front of me there were a metal desk and two metal chairs. I was sitting in a chair. I tried to pull my hands to my face but felt burning around my wrists so I stopped. I tried to stand up but felt the same burning around my ankles. I wriggled around and realized my hands were tied behind my back and my ankles were tied together. I tried to call out for help but my lips felt like they were glued shut. Holy shit, there was tape on my mouth!

My heartbeat started working overtime as panic began to set in. My eyes darted all over the room as I tried to pull my hands free from their bindings. I could feel the rope burning and cutting into my skin so I had to stop. I felt sweat forming around the tape on my mouth and I realized how thirsty I was. Calm down. Breathe. I took a few deep breaths but the sound of a door opening behind me made my breath come to a screaming halt.

"Hey there, you're awake." I heard footsteps and then saw Lamb standing in front of me. "You're not gonna scream if I take that off your mouth, right? I don't want this to be any harder than it has to be."

I shook my head and narrowed my eyes, trying to kill him with my look.

"Okay then." He pulled slowly at the tape and it felt like he was tearing my skin off. He stepped back.

"What the fuck do you think you're doing?" I screeched, the words burning as they tore up my dry throat. I lunged forward but went nowhere. I winced at the pain in my wrists.

He quickly slapped a hand over my mouth. "Hey now, you promised no screaming. I'll put this back on if you don't play nice." He stood there, waving the piece of tape at me. I remained quiet. "That's my girl" He removed his hand.

"Don't call me that."

"That's fine. I know you're pretty pissed at me. Can you please just sit still while I try to explain?" He walked over to the desk and sat on the edge. "Now, first off I wanna start by saying how sorry I am that my guy hurt you. He took it upon himself to do that; it was never my intention."

"Let me go!"

"I can't do that. Not yet. Not until I talk to you and I know you're not going to run. You were bleeding pretty bad - the whole thing went to shit." He looked down into his hands. "I heard your cell phone ring and my friend took matters into his own hands. We can have this all cleared up in no time."

I hated him. I wanted to jump up and gouge his eyes out. "Why are you doing this? When my father finds out about this he..."

"Oh your father knows, trust me. He's on his way here right now as a matter of fact. When he found out what you've been up to with your little boyfriend there, well, let's just say he was very disappointed. You made it easy for me, using your Amex business card while you were in California."

What? My father approved of this shit? Did he hate me that much? My head was throbbing in my temples. I felt sick to my stomach all of a sudden. "Please untie me. I don't feel good and I'm thirsty." I dropped my chin to my chest.

"Oh hell," he said, getting up and coming close to me. He picked my chin up with his fingers and squinted while looking in my eyes. "I'll call a doctor then. Sit tight." He disappeared behind me but he left the door open. I could hear more talking. "I'm gonna call Ross to come in here. I think she's got a concussion."

Who was he talking to? Who else was there? I wanted to call out for my father but decided against it. What good would that do since he already knew I was there? I heard footsteps again. I looked up to see Thomas Hawthorne and almost threw up in my lap.

"How are you feeling?"

"Fuck you."

He chuckled and crossed his arms, shaking his head. "Can't tame that mountain lion, can we?" He pulled out the chair behind the desk and sat down. "George is calling a doctor to come in and look you over."

"Then you can untie me."

"I don't think so. Not just yet. You need to calm down first. Can I do anything for you?"

"Yes…I need some water." I hated having to ask him for help but my throat hurt.

He stood up and disappeared behind me. He came back with a bottle of water and held it to my lips. I drank greedily even though it made me feel like a child, sitting there tied up and needing him. Our eyes were locked the entire time. When I got out of this I was going to slap that smirk off his face, the asshole.

I took a few more sips and drank slowly that time. My stomach had begun to churn and I was fighting the urge to vomit. I turned my head away when I had had enough.

"Is that better?"

"Where's my father?"

"He should be here very soon. But he's going to tell you the same thing I'm about to."

"Oh yeah, and what's that?"

"That all you have to do is agree to a few things and you will be out of here in no time." He paused. "In a few days, Lucas Benjamin won't be a threat to us anymore."

Holy fuck…Lucas! I closed my eyes as my heart began to ache. I thought back on the chain of events; I called Lamb for information, Lucas started remembering things, the man I saw following me. I want the detectives who are on the case to know any information I may have, right or wrong, and investigate it. He had been remembering things and telling the detectives at the station. Everything he told the police went right back to Wallace, I was sure of it. I looked to Thomas again.

"Just how many people does Vance Wallace have in his pocket?"

He chuckled. "Oh, you'd be surprised."

"Where is she? I want to see her right now George!" I heard my father's voice. "Oh my God, Jennifer…" He leaned in and started untying my feet. "Can somebody tell me why the hell she's tied up like this?" I heard his voice crack. Angry? He couldn't be crying…no way. He leaned over me and untied my wrists next. I could smell the familiar scent of his aftershave and my stomach tied up in knots. My father; the one who was never around, who shipped me off after my mother died, who treated me less like a daughter every day, was here…coming to my rescue. My head was pounding so badly I wasn't sure what I was seeing anymore.

My arms flopped free at my sides and I brought my hands to my lap. I inspected the bloody rings around my wrists and bile started to build in my throat. I leaned to the side and threw up all over the floor. I felt dizzy and wanted to go to sleep.

"Where the hell is that goddamn doctor?"

"He's on his way."

"I'm taking her to a hospital."

I couldn't sit upright any more. My body felt like lead and I just wanted to lie down. I leaned so I could lay my head down. Just for a few minutes. I just needed a nap. I felt someone put their arms around me. "Lucas…"

Part 2
Lucas

Chapter Fourteen

The sun was high and the air was warm when I left Jen's apartment. Finally some sun. I was sick of cold winds and short days.

I was starving so I stopped for a bagel and orange juice. I wasn't completely comfortable in my new apartment yet so all I had in my fridge was a couple of beers and some peanut butter. Since waking up clueless in the hospital a year ago I hadn't done much with my life except stare at people at the courthouse. It felt good to have a new routine.

My new apartment building was only four blocks from Jen's place. It made me feel more comfortable being closer to her. Plus it was better than the shit hole I had been living in before. This place was clean, made of brick, not crappy cement, plus the elevator worked. While in the elevator on the way to the sixth floor I fumbled around looking for my keys. They weren't in my jeans pockets or my jacket.

The elevator doors opened but I didn't get out. Instead I hit the G button and pulled out my cell to call Jen.

Damn it, no answer. I ended the call when I heard Jen's stern, lawyer-like voice begin with her message, which made me smile. I tapped out a text instead.

U have my keys? I'm coming back.

I double-timed it back the way I came. As I was about to cross the alleyway next to Jen's apartment building, I was almost run over by a car whizzing out. "Hey…" I yelled as I lurched back. The car pulled out, turning left, squealing tires in the process.

I regained my footing and noted how distracted I was. I nodded to the doorman and he touched the brim of his hat with a nod back as I passed him and entered Jen's apartment building. I checked my phone in the elevator…still no response. Finally the doors opened on her floor and I immediately knew something was wrong. Her door wasn't closed all the way.

My heartbeat kicked up a couple of notches and I fell into cop-mode. I instinctively reached for my gun but it wasn't there. Shit! I tip-toed up to the door and listened for any movement. I didn't hear any noise so

I peered in through the small opening. I elbowed the door lightly and it squeaked as it opened an inch further. I waited but there was still no noise or movement. I pushed the door open further with my hand and every muscle in my body tensed as I entered. I took two small steps into the living room and listened.

"Jen?" I called out, my eyes darting from one spot to another. No answer. "I think I left my keys…" Nothing.

I walked through the living room and noticed her phone on the desk next to her laptop. That's strange. Maybe she's in the shower. I walked slowly, skulking like a cat through the apartment. As I approached the kitchen I saw broken glass, water and blood all over the floor and knew Jen was in trouble. I turned and darted to her bedroom, calling out for her.

"Jennifer! Jennifer, where are you?"

I bolted into the room, seeing nothing out of place. No blood anywhere so she obviously hadn't come in here. I poked my head into the bathroom. Where could she be? Where had all that blood come from? She didn't have her cell so someone must have….

I darted to the windows in the front of the apartment and foolishly thought I would see the black sedan that almost ran me over. I knew someone had been there and had taken Jennifer. And something terrible happened in the process. "Shit!" I banged my hand on the window in frustration. I had missed it all by minutes.

I paced around the room as I tried to calm myself down. What did I really know? The door was open, blood on the floor, Jen was gone, the car in the ally. I pulled out my phone.

"MacCabe"

"Mac, it's Lucas. I'm at Jen's and something's happened. It's definitely a crime scene here so you'd better send a crew."

"Whudda mean? What happened?"

"I don't know. I left here about forty-five minutes ago and she was fine. I forgot my keys and when I came back for them I found blood." I rubbed my forehead. "Look, just get your guys over here, okay? I'll wait here for you."

"Alright, sit tight."

I knew it had been a bad idea to be here yesterday, I fucking knew it. I laced my hands behind my head and paced around some more. I was angry with myself for not going with my instincts since Jen had come home. I thought back to when she first walked in the door. She was so beautiful with her hair all mussed up. I remembered her sexy body tangled up around mine. My heart started to ache as my mind clicked over to imagining her somewhere, scared and hurt.

I stood at the window, anxiously looking for Mac. No sign of him. I knew the more time that went by the harder it was going to be to find her. I decided to walk around again and see if there was something I'd missed.

When I re-entered the bedroom I looked around, hands on hips, trying to concentrate on details. I pushed past the image of us making love on the bed and caught sight of my keys on the nightstand. I walked over and grabbed them. There was a red folder on the bench at the end of the bed. I picked it up and opened it. I pulled out pages of notes Jennifer had taken. I sat down and began reading.

I felt sick to my stomach as I read her 'file'. She had gone to California without telling me. I ran a hand through my hair. "What did you do Jen?" I whispered and kept reading. She had various details about a man who ran a business for Wallace. I had never heard of him before. I finished reading and took the file with me out to the living room. I looked around that room next. I saw her laptop and phone. I picked up her phone and checked it. There was just the missed call from me and my text, nothing new. I opened her laptop and her email page was open. I pulled the chair out and sat down. There was an email from the Thomas Hawthorne from the file. Bastard. He might be the one who came here.

Since the front door was still wide open I heard the elevator ding then MacCabe's voice out in the hallway. I closed the computer, keeping the file in my hands, and met him at the door.

"Lucas, what's going on?"

"Thanks for coming. There must have been a struggle - come on, in here."

I led Mac to the kitchen and we both stood in the doorway, assessing the room.

"Did you see anything - hear anything?" he asked.

"No, it was like this when I got here. I didn't see anyone on my way back here either..." I paused as I thought of the car.

"What...what'd you see?" Mac asked.

"There was a black sedan...he almost ran me over when he came out of the alley. I didn't think anything of it at the time - I'm sure it was whoever took her."

"Calm down, you don't know that. It could have been anyone. Did you happen to get a plate on the car?"

I thought back and all I could see was a black flash as I jumped out of his way.

"I didn't see it but I'm sure it was a four-door sedan though."

"Let's see if there are any cameras on the street or surrounding buildings that we can pull up. Anything else?"

"This has Wallace written all over it, you know that, right?"

"What makes you say that?"

"Because it's no coincidence that George Lambert comes to talk to me, asking me all kinds of questions about Jen and me. Then she disappears? Come on…"

"Now wait a second, I don't think George Lambert would be that stupid."

My gut told me something was off. I hadn't said George was the one who had taken Jennifer.

"Lucas?"

"Yeah…well…I just want to find Jen."

"Look, CSI will do a once over on this place and find out whoever's been in here. You know the drill…it'll be fine." He clapped me on the shoulder. "We'll find her."

Mac turned and walked to the living room again. I took the red folder and tucked it into my waistband under my jacket.

"We need a team in the kitchen to start and I want the entire place dusted for prints." I figured I should disappear. I wanted more than anything to take Jen's computer with me but there was no way I was gonna be able to walk out with it. Her apartment was a crime scene now and everything was important. That folder was mine for now.

I walked back to the living room and waited for Mac to finish up with his instructions.

"I'm gonna head home," I said, rubbing the back of my neck. I couldn't stand seeing all the men that were trudging through Jen's apartment; it was unnerving.

"Now wait a sec, I'm gonna want to get a statement from you."

"I don't know anything Mac, I wasn't here."

"What time did you leave here, exactly?"

"It was just after eight I guess, why?"

"And you said you left your keys…" His voice trailed off as he looked around the room and back to me again. "You ever find them?"

"Yeah they were in her room - what's with the interrogation?"

"Are we gonna find your fingerprints?"

My eyebrows shot into my forehead in surprise. "Whudda mean? Of course you will. What's this about – why are you treating me like a suspect?"

"Just make sure you're reachable. I wanna be able to get in touch with you should I have any questions." He turned around and started talking with a forensic tech.

I didn't like being interrogated by Mac - I'd been expecting to help with the investigation. Something was way off. I took the stairs, not wanting to wait for an elevator. When I came out at the lobby my cell rang. I fumbled to answer it.

"Yeah, hello?"

"Lucas Benjamin?"

"Yeah…who's this?"

"This is Phillip Monroe. We need to talk."

Chapter Fifteen

I balled my fist up and a knot of anger formed in my gut. I clenched my jaw to hold back from raging at him.

"What do you want Monroe?" I asked as calmly as I could. I walked out the back door and stood in the alley. I wanted privacy.

"Is there someplace you and I can meet?"

"Why? Why don't you just tell me what you want right now?"

"Where are you right now?"

"I'm where you should be, at Jen's apartment. Did you know your daughter is missing?"

"Look, stop right there. I don't have time to tango with you about all the things I've done wrong, alright?" I heard him sigh and was glad he was frustrated. "I need to talk to you - right now - there isn't any time to waste."

"What do you know about all this? God dammit, if she's hurt I'm go..."

"She's fine."

"Where is she?"

"Lucas, please, right now you have to trust me. I'm not in the mood for games. All I want is for this to be over. So please, can we just meet somewhere?"

I could hear desperation in his voice and considered it was possible that he was reaching out for some kind of help. He knew where Jennifer was but my gut was worried the whole conversation was just a trick to get me killed.

"I know you love her," he said. "I love her too. Please...I need your help."

I kicked a discarded Styrofoam container against the brick wall of the alley, frustrated as hell. I rubbed the back of my neck and looked up at the sky with closed eyes, and tried to clamp down and think. The son of a bitch was playing on my emotions and it pissed me off. Trouble was, I didn't have much choice. I did love Jen and I was desperate to find her, but I needed at least neutral ground where he couldn't pull anything.

"Fine. There's a diner I know of…"

After I gave Monroe directions, I decided that neutral ground wasn't enough. I needed an edge in case things went south and that meant I needed my gun. I hoped to walk off some of my frustration on the way to my place but my mind was racing.

My gut was twisted with guilt that Jen was involved and now eyeballs deep in my shitty mess of a life. I knew I should have just stayed away from people, women in particular. I should have just minded my own business, sitting on that bench concentrating on the faces. Then no one would've gotten hurt. But damn it, she was so beautiful; when she had come into the diner all soaking wet and flustered. When she brought me that coffee I knew then that I was falling in love with her. No one paid any mind to me, and for a long time I liked it that way. If it weren't for Jen, I would never have found a day job, switched apartments, never would have actually wanted to go somewhere other than the diner to eat. I would never have had any memories without her either.

I couldn't help but wonder what Jen's dad wanted to talk to me about or what kind of help I could possibly provide for him. What if it was just a trap? What if Vance Wallace was waiting instead of Monroe? Would he tell me he killed my parents? Would he even remember who they were? Phillip Monroe knew who I was and he knew about Jen and me so I was pretty positive that Wallace knew too. It had to be a trap.

I ran up the back stairs into my building and up to my apartment. I wasn't supposed to have a gun now. They'd taken my service weapon when I'd been transferred off the force, but somehow they'd missed my backup, an old Colt 1911 that my dad had carried in the war. I pulled the file from my waistband, stashed it behind the most godawful painting ever made that hung over the mantel and shoved the pistol into my jacket pocket. I hoped I wouldn't need it but I just couldn't trust Monroe.

Phillip was already waiting for me when I arrived at the diner. He was in the last booth in the back.

"Well hey there stranger," Gerry said as I walked past her.

"Hey Gerry," I said flatly.

"Thanks for coming," Phillip said. "I wasn't sure you would show up."

He was finely dressed in a suit and tie, looking cool and reserved. I wanted to punch him in his condescending face. "Where is she?"

"In a warehouse at the dock. She has a concussion and a pretty bad laceration on her arm. There was a doctor with her when I left."

"The address." My eyes never left his. I felt sick to my stomach at the thought of Jen being hurt.

He actually squirmed under my gaze. "I want her home too, believe me. But you can't just walk in there then walk back out with her on your arm. It's not going to work that way."

"Well, tell me then - how do you think this is all going to work?"

"If Jennifer is going to make it out of this I'm going to need your help. But first there are some things you should know."

"If you mean that Vance Wallace is behind this, I already know. And I already know that you're his lawyer too. So let's get to the part where you tell me where Jen is and I call the police."

"You really need to stop talking to the police, Lucas."

"I'm sure you and Wallace would love that." I sat back and slid my hand into the pocket that held my gun.

"Why do you think Jennifer is where she is right now? Think about it. The last thing you told your detective friend was that you were suspicious of George Lambert. Now George has taken it upon himself to take Jennifer to use her as bait to get to you."

He was right; the last thing I'd told Mac was about George Lambert. But how did Phillip know that? I thought back to all the other things that I had told Mac, starting from when I was at the beach house with Jen. I had told him that I remembered who Vance Wallace was. The next thing was about George. After that there was always someone following Jen, including the night we went out for pizza. Could Mac be relaying information to Wallace? He had to have been. That would explain why he was asking me those questions at Jen's apartment. He was probably trying to figure out how much I knew about her disappearance. The less I knew the better it would be to use me as bait. Mac knew how I felt about Jen, and Wallace was gonna use it against me; the very thing I was afraid of all along. "Oh my God, this is all my fault."

"I could say the same thing."

"How did you know I told anything at all to the police?"

"You have no idea just how many people Mr. Wallace knows in this town." He steepled his fingers and leaned towards me. "He's been threatening me for years and I'm ready to be done with it." He sat back again, appraising my reaction.

I didn't have a reaction because I'd seen it a million times; some guy gets too big for his britches and thinks he owns everyone. Guys like that do whatever it takes to keep themselves feeling powerful. Wallace was no different. "So what do you want from me?"

"You're close to the police. And you're the only person I can trust to do the right thing for my daughter." He looked down and started fiddling with his hands with a grim look on his face.

"I don't know how I'm supposed to help. You said yourself I can't just barge in and take Jen outta there."

Gerry came to our table, interrupting our conversation. "Can I get you gentleman something to drink?"

"Thanks Gerry…maybe I'll have some coffee."

"Nothing for me, thanks," Monroe said, not looking up. It made me think he was avoiding contact in case she was asked about it later. Or maybe he was just an arrogant asshole, I wasn't sure.

Gerry was back in a flash with my coffee and the small jug of cream. "If you need anything you just let me know, k?"

"Thanks, I will."

I added cream to my coffee and began stirring. "Maybe I should give Wallace what he wants and just let him kill me."

"That's not what's best for Jennifer. She loves you."

I was surprised.

"So what then…how do we get her outta there?"

"Seeing as I'm the attorney for most of the men that are at that warehouse right now, I can't tell you much of anything."

I laughed. "It's a little late for you to be thinking about obeying the law of attorney client privilege now, isn't it?"

"I have to maintain that if the evidence we get is to stand up in court. But what I can do is get them to incriminate themselves, give them enough rope to hang themselves."

"What do you mean?"

"First let me ask you - is there anyone at the police station that you trust? I know you thought you could trust your old partner, but could there be anyone else?"

I laughed. "Why don't you tell me who Wallace doesn't have on his payroll and we'll start that way."

"What about Sergeant Brentzel?"

I considered it for a moment. I hadn't directly spoken to my sergeant about all this. Only because Mac had assured me he'd take care of it, that it would sound better coming from him. I was willing to bet Sarge didn't know a thing. "He would be my first choice."

"My thought was to go back in to the warehouse wearing a wire. I would talk to Thomas Hawthorne."

"Who is this Hawthorne guy?" I asked.

"He's an associate of Mr. Wallace; someone who has developed a bit of an ego. I would like to see if I can get him to say something that would give the police cause to arrest him."

"Something like what?"

"About the business that he runs."

I thought back to the file that Jen had and I remembered reading a note she had written in the margin - he ran a shipping business for Wallace. It had to be the drugs. What better way to get them brought here than through your own company. "Who is this Hawthorne anyway? Why talk to him and not George?"

"He's a close associate of Mr. Wallace. And he's a bit loose at the lips; something George would never be."

That made sense. I started to wonder why I had never heard of Thomas Hawthorne or this shipping business from my time undercover. Maybe that's one of the things I couldn't remember. That was possible but it could also be something new Wallace was doing now; something the police didn't even know about. I had known he was running drugs but I never did find out where they came from.

"Okay, so let's say this Hawthorne is stupid enough to get himself arrested and sings like a canary. All Wallace will do is panic - what if he kills Jen just to save his own ass?"

"The key is to arrest Thomas quietly. And the first thing he'll do is call me. But I'll be conveniently tied up doing something else, unreachable maybe, I don't know. Until I arrive, he'll need to be pushed. He'll slip…I know Thomas."

I could tell he didn't like the guy, not just by the eye roll but because of the way he had reached for a napkin and was twisting it into a thin line.

"I'm gonna have to set up a meeting with Sarge and I'm not sure how easy that's gonna be after what happened this morning. MacCabe will no doubt start tailing me."

"Detective MacCabe will certainly put us at a disadvantage." His cell phone began to ring. He pulled it out of the breast pocket of his jacket and looked at it. "I have to take this, excuse me." He stood up and walked to the front of the diner. "Phillip Monroe. Yes…"

Dammit Mac. It pissed me off that my partner, my best friend, was working for the guy we, or at least I, had worked tirelessly to bust. The guy killed my parents for Christ's sake. I wondered if it was the money that made working for Wallace so enticing. Then I started to wonder how long he had been going behind my back.

Phillip came back to the table. "Jennifer's awake. She's doing better."

"How do you know that? Who were you talking to?"

"It was George. I asked him to call me when Jennifer woke up."

"So you're in contact with the people who have her? What else are you discussing with them?" I said, looking around. I half expected a bunch of guys to come in and grab me and take me to the warehouse with Jen. "How am I supposed to believe anything you're saying to me?"

"I can understand why you would think that, but what choice do you have? What choice have I? I can't think of a better way to get her back alive, can you?"

I didn't like it, but he was right. I made a promise to myself, if he was double-dealing me now and Jen got hurt, he was a dead man.

"She's probably going out of her mind in there."

"The quicker you can get me wired the quicker we can get her out."

"What does Wallace have on you anyway? You said he was threatening you."

He picked up the napkin again and began twisting it. "Mr. Wallace is someone to be taken very seriously. When he says he's going to do something you can count on it. I learned the hard way just how serious he is."

I pictured Wallace having control over his firm or something. Maybe Phillip was hiding drugs there, who knew? Right then I didn't really care; I only cared about getting Jen. "I'll reach out to Sarge then. He's gonna love meeting you."

"Make the call."

Chapter Sixteen

I sat anxiously in the back of an undercover van with Sergeant Brentzel. We were parked three blocks from the warehouse where Jen was being held. It was hot and stuffy in the van so I opened a bottle of water and took a couple of slugs. We were both wearing headphones, listening as Phillip drove to the warehouse. Sarge was giving Phillip last minute instructions and trying to calm his nerves. Since I wasn't legally a police officer, I wasn't technically supposed to be a part of what was happening. I promised like a good boy scout to keep my mouth shut and my backside planted in the seat.

I listened, half-heartedly, while Phillip asked questions and Sarge answered like a coach trying to toughen up his best quarterback before the championship game. I rolled my eyes and pulled my headphones off, letting them drape around my neck. I leaned back and stretched my legs, thinking that less than twenty-four hours ago Phillip was all gung-ho and determined to do whatever it took to get Jen out of that warehouse. I was sick of hearing him whine like a baby about it when it was finally time to man up.

I leaned on my knees and sighed. Give him a break. He didn't like having Jen locked up like a prisoner any more than I did. He was willing to risk his life and career to free her, which was more than I was doing at the moment. He was entitled to be a little nervous.

After Phillip and I had talked at the diner, we had met up with Sergeant Brentzel in an isolated area at Central Park. Phillip did most of the talking and I verified his story. I also told Sarge about the file that Jen had put together. I explained my theory about Wallace and Hawthore shipping drugs in and out; that the other men from the file who were scattered around the city must have been storing or possibly selling the drugs from their location. Phillip told Sarge that Detective MacCabe was working for Vance Wallace and had been for at least the past six months. I was relieved that Mac hadn't been going behind my back while we were partners. Sarge had been less than thrilled to get all the info from us and didn't waste any time with forming a plan. He agreed to go along with the idea of wiring Phillip, but first he had to take care of Mac. Once Mac was no longer a threat Sarge would contact us again.

That night I had a bad dream. I was in a burning building and I saw Vance Wallace with a gun pointed at me. He had a grin on his face.

It wasn't until just before noon the next day that Sarge finally called, saying he had the go-ahead on Philip's plan. He didn't mention Mac and I figured it better not to ask. I knew he was pissed that so much had happened right under his nose.

The three of us met up again to put the wire on Phillip. Phillip insisted we not worry about a wire being detected but Sarge was still pretty uptight about it, saying he didn't want any screw ups. Phillip repeated himself many times saying that he wasn't in any danger and he didn't care what happened to him anyway. Sarge secured the wiring device around his torso and velcroed everything in place. After Phillip was buttoned back up they did a few sound checks to make sure the quality was good, then Phillip tucked a small device in his ear that would allow him to hear Sarge. Lastly, Sarge put a small chip behind the lapel of Phillip's jacket which would provide a GPS location should something go wrong.

"Hey, you okay?" Sarge said, giving my shoulder a pat with the back of his hand, bringing me back to the present.

I ran my hand through my hair with a sigh. "Yeah, just worried."

"He's almost there so you should put your cans back on."

I put my headphones back on and heard the sound of the wind rushing in through Phillip's open car window. I wanted to tell him not to screw it up and to just get in and get out, but Sarge had already told him that. I felt worthless, just sitting there wringing my hands with nothing better to do than to listen.

"I'm pulling in," Phillip said in a muted voice.

My stomach twisted as I envisioned all the things that could possibly go wrong. I felt the sweat bead up on my forehead as my heart beat a steady rhythm in my temples.

"Just stick to the plan and I'll let you know when we have enough to arrest Hawthorne," Sarge said to Phillip. "You're sure he's gonna be there?"

"Yes, he'll be here. He has a sick notion that he and Jennifer have a budding relationship." After a pause he softly said, "I'm sorry Lucas."

My hands were already balled up into fists and my lips set in a tight line so the apology didn't register. Keep it together I reminded myself. I knew from Jen's notes in the file that she was repulsed by him so it wasn't her I was worried about. It was that sleaze-ball Hawthorne. With Jen locked up and possibly being threatened, who knew what he'd try to get her to do.

I shook the thought out of my head and listened as I heard a heavy metal door creak open and slam shut. Footsteps echoed as Phillip made his way through the warehouse. I could hear voices in the distance, becoming louder as Phillip approached them.

"How is she?"

"She's fine. Ross said she'd have a bad headache for a while and to keep an eye on her. He stitched up her arm too. She's in pain but she won't take the pills Ross left."

"I'd like to see her now."

I heard footsteps and shuffling and then a door opened.

"You can leave, George. I'd like to be alone with her please."

"Dammit, what's he doing? This isn't part of the plan," Sarge said, chewing the tip of his thumb.

"What do you want?" I leaned in closer as I heard Jen's clipped words break the silence. My heart pounded and I thought I would choke as a knot formed in my throat.

"I wanted to see you - make sure you were alright."

"Alright? I'm anything but alright. Are you gonna get me out of here?"

Silence. "I can't do that right now. I…"

"Why the hell not?"

There were footsteps and then the sound of metal being pulled across the floor…a chair? I heard Phillip sigh heavily and I wondered if he was struggling with telling her what he was up to; that he was wired. Was he giving her a signal? Was he showing her the wire? The suspense was unnerving.

"What's going on Daddy? What are you involved in with Vance Wallace?"

"You'll know the truth eventually. I need for you to trust me right now. Please."

"I don't know how I'm supposed to do that." I heard her sniff and imagined she was crying or maybe fighting the urge. "Lucas tried to warn me about all this shit and I wouldn't listen."

"Lucas is a good man."

"How would you know anything about being a good man? You associate with liars and kidnappers." Now I was sure she was crying. "You can tell me all you want that it's just your job but you and I both know that's bullshit. You've gone way too far past just doing your job. Maybe that helps you sleep at night but I don't buy it."

"I know I haven't been a good father to you. I know I've made some mistakes, but…"

"Some mistakes? Why don't you try years of mistakes? Shipping me off like that after Mom died - and treating me like shit ever since! Now I'm somewhere against my will, taken by someone you know, and you won't get me out of here. Guess actions speak louder than words, huh Dad."

"Jennifer I…"

"Just get out."

"Please. If you'll ju…"

"Leave!"

I heard shuffling and then his footsteps. The door opened and closed softly. He sighed and then was walking again.

"Where's Thomas?" Phillip asked someone.

"In the upstairs office," George answered.

I heard Phillip's footsteps clanging up a flight of stairs. The sweat on my forehead was now trickling down past my ears. Every muscle in my body was tense and tight.

"Phillip," said Hawthorne. "Come in - sit down."

There was classical music playing in the office as Phillip walked further in. Stick to the plan, Phillip.

"Just how long does George plan on keeping Jennifer here?" Phillip asked.

"You'll have to ask him that. If it were up to me she'd be in a hotel where she could be comfortable and have the best food available."

My stomach churned and bile filled my throat. I wanted to kill him.

"She shouldn't be a part of this at all."

"I agree with you," Hawthorne said. "You and I are on the same page here so don't make me out to be the bad guy. George has been trying to convince her, unsuccessfully, to call Lucas Benjamin."

Guilt welled up; she was trying to protect me.

"Why are you even here Thomas?

"I'm here because I care about what happens to Jennifer. And I can do my business from here, you know that."

"Why do you suddenly care so much about Jennifer? What's going on between you two?"

"George called me a few days ago—said your daughter was in town and for me to check on her—see what she was up to. I just assumed she knew about the business."

"Well, what's the newest information you have? Because I won't have time to fix any of your mistakes." Phillips tone was condescending. Finally, he was on topic. I heard a chair move and then footsteps. I assumed Thomas didn't appreciate being called incompetent and pictured him needing to pace off his frustrations. Prick.

"The next shipment leaves California tonight and should be here in New York by morning. It's probably a good thing I'm here; that way I can meet the shipment when it arrives. Mr. Wallace will be pleased with this new product I've arranged."

"That's it, we got him," Sarge said. "Wrap it up and come on out."

I pictured Thomas standing there with his chest all puffed out, hands on his hips and a 'take that' look on his face. The dummy didn't know it but he was bragging himself right into an arrest.

"What's the new product?" Phillip asked.

"Careful here, Phil. Don't push it," Sarge said, bouncing his foot up and down.

"Mr. Wallace has been saying that his usual product wasn't pure enough and that he wanted to get a new supplier. I heard through a connection there was something new coming from Columbia and he could arrange for me to get some. The cost was the same…this time anyway. And that was no small chore convincing the man but I managed. This cocaine should be to Mr. Wallace's liking. I sampled the product myself."

"More than enough," Sarge said.

"Fine then. I'm going to head to my office for a few hours. Call my cell if you need to reach me."

"I'll take care of Jennifer, don't worry, okay? I won't let what happened to Patricia happen to her."

I could almost hear the smile on Thomas Hawthorne's face when he said it. I wanted to bust out of that van and go break his neck. My teeth were clenched tight. I pulled the headphones off and threw them against the wall of the van.

"We've got him, Lucas. This will be over soon," Sarge said. "Phillip, we'll meet you at your office. We're gonna need you to do one more thing."

Sarge pulled his headphones off and clambered through the van and into the driver's seat. I wanted so badly to get out of there. Big rings of sweat had formed in my shirt under my arms and around my neck. My head was pounding and I just wanted to punch a hole in something. I didn't know how much longer I could wait to get Jen out of that warehouse. I considered going there that night. I'd wait until late when everyone would be sleeping. I'd slip in, kill whoever got in my way and take Jen home.

"You comin' up here or what?"

"Yeah, yeah," I said, getting up and climbing into the passenger seat.

I thought back to the last thing Thomas Hawthorne had said. Who was Patricia?

Chapter Seventeen

We drove to Phillip's office in silence.

I was sure Sarge was running through all the steps of what would happen next; making sure every detail was just right so nothing could be questioned later. That's what I would have been doing. I couldn't stop thinking about Jen and how upset she had been while she was talking to her father. All I wanted was to get her out of there and tell her everything was gonna be okay. But I couldn't do that because I was stuck playing Boy Scout, forced to sit on the sidelines and watch. I felt incompetent and worthless doing jack shit to help.

Phillip was already waiting for us. I felt an eerie sense of déjà vu being in the place where Jen worked; so close to the place I had sat for almost a year. Phillip was standing with his hands in the pockets of his slacks staring out the floor to ceiling window. I wondered if he was considering jumping.

"That was pretty gutsy of you back there," Sarge said, after closing the door.

"I didn't want to leave anything to question his arrest." Phillip's voice was deadpan. He turned to face us. "What is it you need me to do next?"

"I'll need you to call Hawthorne and tell him to come here. We can't arrest him at the warehouse so we need to get him out of there somehow."

"Fine. Anything else?"

"Yeah," I said taking a few steps closer to him. "Who's Patricia?"

He shuffled back a step or two, clearly not expecting the question. After a moment he cleared his throat and walked over to the chair behind his desk. He slumped down and slouched back. His gaze was on a photo on his desk. "Patricia was my wife."

I could feel the blood drain out of my face as I pieced together what little I knew of Jen's mom and combined it with what Thomas Hawthorne had said. "The car crash was no accident, was it?"

"No, it wasn't." He closed his eyes and pinched the bridge of his nose. After a moment he sat up straight in his chair and composed himself.

"Mr. Wallace was sending me a message."

"What do you mean?" My heart went out to the guy. I knew exactly how he felt since I had been sent the same message myself.

"When I first met Vance he was young and cocky. I was his lawyer; he was arrested for various drug charges. But the more powerful he became, the bigger his head got. He wanted me to start going to California to represent other…associates of his whenever they got arrested. At first it was just business as usual for me and I enjoyed the extra money. My wife had just given birth to Jennifer and I was happy to be able to give them anything they would ever need or want."

He stood up and went back to the window. "Vance's business became bigger every year and he was expecting me to do more and more for him. Patricia was always telling me I worked too much and she just wanted me home more. I wanted that as well but Vance wasn't interested. When I finally told him I was dropping him as a client he started threatening me; telling me he would ruin my career and the business I had built. I absolutely believed he was capable of that so I continued working for him. I worried about how I would support my family if I couldn't practice law." He looked down at his shoes.

"So if you stayed, then why did he…do what he did?"

"Once George became involved in Vance's business it became harder and harder to do anything without Vance knowing about it. George used to be my greatest ally. Not too long after we got out of law school we started this business together. We didn't know what the hell we were doing or who the bad guys were. But all that money was too glamorous for George to pass up. He became a different person. He started keeping tabs on me for Vance, even set up people to report back when I was in California. Patricia was getting more and more agitated as every year went by and I was less available. One day she went cleaning in my den at our house and found files I had on shipments coming and going in California. She confronted me with what she had found and threatened to leave me if I didn't quit. I was almost relieved she had found the files. I saw it as my ticket out."

I saw Phillip differently as he spoke. His voice was distant, as though he was in another world while his memories did the talking. He had loved his family and had been trying to do the right thing for them and to keep them protected. I wondered if I would have done anything different had it been me.

"What I didn't know was just how low George would stoop. I had promised Patricia I would quit. I told her that she and I and Jennifer would do as she had always wanted and move to the beach; finally live as a family. I was happy for the first time in years and was looking forward to being with them." A smile swept over his lips but just as quickly disappeared. His eyebrows pushed together as his voice went a notch lower. "George had my house bugged so my whole conversation with Patricia was heard by Vance. He didn't like it when people went behind his back and created problems for him. The next morning I got a call from the police saying that Patricia had been in a car accident and she was in critical condition."

"She was alive?"

"For a while…on life support. Jennifer had been in the car as well but she was fine…just a bit banged up. She has no memory of it." He paused and looked up at me, knowing Jennifer and I had more in common than I realized "When I arrived at the hospital the doctors told me that Patricia had no brain activity and the machine was the only thing keeping her alive." He sniffed and took a breath. "The worst part was that she was six months pregnant. She was on her way home from the doctor."

He covered his eyes with one of his hands and began quietly sobbing. I couldn't imagine that he had spoken about any of this to anyone. How could he, since it might get them killed? Talking about it was probably like reopening a wound. Sarge and I looked at each other, knowing that such things were possible. We had seen it over and over in our line of work.

Phillip started sniffing and taking deep breaths. He folded his arms and continued. "After Patricia was laid to rest my main focus was to keep Jennifer protected. I changed her last name to Callahan, which was Patricia's maiden name, and wanted her as far away from what was going on as possible. The best way I could think of to do that was to send her to school away from the city. Of course Jennifer saw that as me shipping her off because I didn't love her or didn't want to be her father." He turned to face us. "But that was the farthest thing from the truth. Once she was old enough and told me she wanted to be a lawyer like me I was both proud and scared to death. The next best idea I had was to have her here so I could keep a close eye on her and make sure she never got involved with Vance." He walked back over to his desk and sat down. "George took on the role of father figure with her. I had missed so many years and didn't know what she needed. Plus every time I looked at her I saw Patricia. She looks so much like her mother…" His voice trailed off.

"Weren't you worried George would bring up the idea with Jen about working with Wallace?" I asked.

"George had come to love Jennifer like his own daughter. He hadn't been expecting Vance to kill Patricia. His penance was to watch out for Jennifer and keep her safe. At first I allowed it because George saw what Patricia's death did to me. If I lost Jennifer too…what he's doing now - he thinks he's keeping Jennifer safe in some sick, twisted way."

"Jennifer told me Lamb was like a father to her. You knew what he did to your wife - how could you allow a man like that to get so close to your daughter? You put her right smack dab in the middle of potential danger by giving her a job with you. I'm sorry, but if anyone's to blame for where Jennifer is right now, it's you," I said, stabbing a finger at him.

"All of this has gotten way out of control. If we don't start taking some action quick, Wallace is gonna start taking matters into his own hands," Sarge said. He stood up. "Call Hawthorne now and let's get this show on the road. I don't want anyone else to die."

❧

Twenty minutes later I was back in the van with Sarge. We hadn't spoken about what Phillip had revealed up in his office. But I was beginning to think I should be wearing rubber boots so I could easily wash off all the shit I kept stepping in.

An unmarked car pulled up to the curb in front of us. Sarge had called for backup for the arrest of Thomas Hawthorne. It was important to get Thomas inside the building and off the street in order to keep the arrest quiet. We didn't want there to be any attention that would leak back to the warehouse.

It wasn't long before a black Towne car arrived and a man in a well-tailored suit got out of the back. So that's him. He pulled his coat tight and buttoned it before making his way to the door of Phillip's building. As he was walking, two detectives got out of the unmarked car and met him at the door.

"What the hell are they doing?" Sarge asked.

Thomas took his sunglasses off and looked around at his surroundings before nodding his head. No you're not being punked, you stupid prick. One of the detectives cuffed him and was reading him his rights as he escorted Thomas to the car. I smiled.

Sarge started up the van. "That was anything but how I wanted those pricks to arrest him. Dammit, they were supposed to wait until he was inside." He put the van in gear and turned to me. "I want you to have another talk with that police shrink. I'm gonna need some good guys back on my team."

"Yeah" I said, not knowing how I felt about that. "So what's next? What's the plan on getting Jen?"

"First we need to find out how many men are in that warehouse. After that we can get a team together and go in."

"I wanna be on the team."

"Now Lucas, you know that's not possible. You don't have a shield anymore...we need to do this by the book."

I knew he was right but that didn't mean I had to like it. I was frustrated as hell just sitting on my hands.

"Look, you can ride along but you have to promise to stay in the background. I can't have anything go wrong again. We've worked too hard and too long to get this guy."

I was willing to take what I could get. The longer Jen stayed trapped the more anxious I became.

Sarge's phone went off. "Sergeant Brentzel...yeah...and? Dammit." He looked at me then back to the road. "Okay, don't do anything. I'll call you back." He put the phone down and sighed. "That was Phillip. There's a problem."

Chapter Eighteen

After Thomas Hawthorne was arrested, the driver of the Towne car called Lamb to report what had happened. The detectives who arrested Hawthorne apparently had no understanding of what it meant to arrest someone quietly. Once Lamb found out, he called Phillip, suspicious as hell as to what was going on. The whole thing was a cluster fuck and my anxiety was building.

When Sarge and I finally made it to the station, Hawthorne had been put in an interrogation room and told to sit tight. I was leaning against the wall watching Hawthorne through the two-way mirror. He was sitting cool and collected at the table, looking at his fingernails. My breathing picked up. I wanted to walk in there and bust him in his face and pound the shit out of him.

"Hey," Sarge said, clapping me on the shoulder, making me jump. "I'm gonna head in there and see what I can get out of him. Phillip said he'll stall as long as he can." I didn't answer him or turn my gaze away from Hawthorne. "Hey, did you hear me?"

"Yeah, I heard you."

Sarge went in and I planted my feet wide, arms tightly folded. I watched Hawthorne lean back and grin. Sarge sat in one of the chairs across from him, his back to me, and laid a manila folder on the table.

"I have nothing to say until my lawyer arrives,"

"I understand that," Sarge said. "I just have a waiver for you to sign saying you understand your rights and all." He opened the folder in front of him and began shuffling through the papers. "What are you even doing here in New York, Mr. Hawthorne?"

Silence.

"You're from Los Angeles, right?"

Silence. Sarge continued flipping through the folder.

"Do you understand why you were arrested?"

"Look, I hate for you to waste your time, but as I said, I'll wait for my lawyer." Hawthorne crossed his legs and folded his hands in his lap. His confidence wasn't wavering in the least.

"I understand. No harm in asking where you live, right? You need a drink or something?"

"Thank you, no."

"Well, who knows how long your lawyer will be. Security is a bitch to get through. If you need something to eat or drink, I'm happy to have something brought in."

The look on Hawthorne's face changed. The confident prick-grin disappeared. He cleared his throat and shuffled in his chair. "Maybe a cup of coffee, but my lawyer said he would be here as quickly as he could, so I expect him any time now."

"Sure thing," Sarge said, getting up. He opened the door and I heard him ask someone to bring in a cup of coffee. A few moments later the coffee was delivered and Hawthorne took a sip.

"Ugh. This is coffee?"

"Sorry, but that's all we got."

"This is all such a waste of my time," Hawthorne said.

"We take our laws seriously here in the city. I don't know how things are run down there in California but you made a mistake by bringing your drugs here."

Thomas laughed. "You have no idea who you're dealing with. Mr. Wallace is on his way here now and, trust me, when he finds out that I'm here those drugs will be the last thing you'll be worried about."

I couldn't believe it. The stupid prick had done exactly what Phillip had said he would do. He'd incriminated himself and Wallace in the process. But Hawthorne had also said Wallace was on his way. Holy shit…Jen!

I met Sarge in the hallway as he was coming out of the room. He took me by the arm and led me to his office and shut the door.

"Don't even think about it, Lucas."

"How can you say that? You know Wallace is going straight to that warehouse and I'll be damned if I'm gonna just sit ba…"

"Yes, you are gonna just sit back and do nothing."

"Fuck!" I ran my hands through my hair then knotted my fingers behind my head, closed my eyes and tried to slow down my breathing. All I could see was Jen sitting at that warehouse, hurt, pissed off…scared as hell. I was sure she was wondering why no one was helping her. Lamb had betrayed her, her father, and then of course there was me. Had it not been for me she never would have gone digging around in California trying to help me figure my shit out. Everything was so fucked up and it was my fault. There was no way I could sit on the sidelines any more.

Sarge picked up his phone. "Sit," he said. I sighed heavily and complied.

"Phil, this is Sergeant Brentzel. You were right, Hawthorne has a big mouth. There's a problem. Wallace is on his way to New York. Yeah… okay….okay….I'll see, just come in now."

Sarge hung up the phone and directed his attention back to me. "You good?"

If I wanted to continue to be a part of everything I had to act like I had my wits about me, even though that was the farthest thing from the truth. "Yeah, good. What did Phillip have to say?"

"He wants to go back in with a wire. He thinks he can finish all of this and talk to Wallace."

I shuffled in my chair, trying my hardest to keep some semblance of composure. I was agitated as hell knowing that was gonna be a huge waste of time. Wallace wasn't the kind of man who negotiated. He was on his way to remedy a problem and that meant killing Jen.

"It might not be a bad idea, the more I think about it. Maybe Phil can go in there, stall Wallace a bit. Then we can get a team surrounding the place and put all of this to rest once and for all." Sarge said.

"You make it sound so simple. What if Jen is already dead by the time Phillip gets there? Wallace isn't stupid; he's gonna smell bullshit in a heartbeat."

"That may be true but what other choice do we have right now? I can't think of a better idea, can you?"

I couldn't.

"I'm gonna call the DA and get things moving. When Phillip gets here we'll wire him back up and get right back out to the warehouse." He stood up and walked around to the front of his desk. "We're gonna get her out of there, I promise."

I appreciated his words but still wasn't convinced he was right. I didn't have a choice but to go along with what he'd decided. He was running the show and I was lucky to still be involved at all. I felt worthless and naked without my shield. I wasn't sure how much more I could stand. I had to believe she would be brought out safe and I wanted to be there when it happened.

It seemed like an eternity before Sarge and I were back in the van listening as Phillip drove into the warehouse. I was chomping at the bit to hear Jen's voice again and know she was at least still alive. Phillip hadn't even talked to Hawthorne at the station which made me think he was taking the situation very seriously.

I was sure some people would think this whole thing was crazy. Why bother? I could hear them asking me. Why risk my life, my career, my sanity? Why not just get my life back and move on? That was easy; because I loved her. I loved Jen with everything I had left in my heart. She was all I had left in the shitty thing called my life. My parents were dead, my job was gone and I was half a person searching for something to make me whole again. For just a second I had been…her and I together, making love, our hearts tangled just as much as our bodies. I'd be damned if I'd let anything happen to her.

"I'm here."

Phillips voice jolted me back to reality. I took a deep breath and rolled my head back and forth, trying to untangle the tension in my neck. Here we go.

I heard the familiar sound of the heavy metal door squeak open and slam shut. His footsteps echoed through the warehouse, making my heart kick up to a steady rhythm knowing he would soon be in the room where Jen was.

"I don't see anyone," Phillip said quietly.

"Are you sure anyone is still there?" Sarge asked.

Philip didn't answer but his footsteps continued. There was a knock on a door. The door opened.

"What the hell are you doing here?" I recognized Lamb's voice.

"I came here to see my daughter - I shouldn't need an appointment! Let me in…"

"Yeah, let him in Lamb."

Immediately I knew the other voice belonged to Vance Wallace. The sarcasm in his voice filled my ears like a siren. I balled my hands into fists and felt the blood pounding in my ears.

"Jennifer…are you okay?"

"Yeah, peachy."

I released my fists and snapped to attention, relieved to hear her voice. Considering all that was going on she still had a snarky attitude. Careful Jen.

"Welcome to the party," Wallace said. "I was just in the process of discussing a new job description for your daughter. Seems like now would be a good time to teach her the full extent of the family business, don't 'cha think?"

"This is madness. I want you to let her go. She has nothing to do with this."

Wallace laughed. I started cracking my knuckles.

"That's a good one Phil. You really are a dumb fuck, you know that? First of all, this bitch ain't goin' nowhere. And second, if she does walk outta here, it won't be unless she's on my payroll."

"I would never work for you, you fucking asshole!"

"Whew, she's feisty. Mm mm mm...I like that. I like that a lot."

"Get your fucking hands off me..."

My face was burning with fury and sweat was dripping down the back of my neck. Wallace was laughing again. It was taking all of my willpower to keep my ass planted.

"She has your attitude. But it's not completely inflexible, is it Phil? See if you can change her mind. Or I'll change it for her - just like I changed yours."

"What's he talking about?" Jen asked. I squeezed my eyes shut.

"Oh, this just gets better by the second. You mean she doesn't know?"

"Don't."

"No you don't." He wasn't laughing anymore. "I don't know who you think you are but you work for me. I call the shots around here. I'm runnin' out of patience...I'm sick of this bullshit. What's it gonna be? Huh?"

It was silent and the only thing I could hear was my heart pounding in my ears. My eyes darted around at the equipment in front of me but I wasn't really seeing any of it. My mind's eye was picturing the room, trying to figure out what everyone was doing.

"Maybe you need some incentive," Wallace said slowly.

My head exploded as the sound of a gunshot pierced through my headphones. The next thing I heard was Jen screaming. Holy shit! I tore my headphones off and bounded out the back of the van.

"Lucas, wait!"

I didn't stop. My mind was made up. I was at a full sprint running to

Part 3

The Warehouse

Chapter Nineteen

Jennifer

It was the afternoon. I could tell because the streaks of sunlight on the warehouse floor were becoming longer and the breeze coming in the huge windows from the bay had gotten chilly. The room I'd been kept in since I'd been brought to the warehouse was just an unused office. The enormous floor to ceiling windows that gave me a life-line to the outside world were far above the water of the bay, so I couldn't get out through them. I was trapped like a caged animal. And every time Lamb came in it was as if he was poking that caged animal. It only got worse when my father showed up.

My father…he had some nerve; coming in trying to be all conciliatory with me. Once again he was looking out only for himself and didn't give a damn about me. Which was fine. I was done. I'd had it. If there was one good thing about being locked in a room alone, it was that I had a lot of time to think. And I thought about a lot of things. The first thing I planned to do when I got out was to pack up my office and tell my father to fuck off. I was smart. I was more than capable of making it on my own somewhere else. I was sick of him beating me down and making me feel inadequate.

The other thing I thought about was Lucas. I pictured his face and tried my hardest to remember every detail. I probably made up a few things but I didn't care. His face kept me strong…kept me going. The night we had finally made love was an image I played out over and over; his touch, his words, his kisses. All I needed were his arms around me. I promised myself when I finally got out of there I would tell him how much I loved him. Tell him how sorry I was I had gone behind his back to California and was probably putting him through hell.

But did Lucas even know I was missing? We were supposed to have only limited contact with each other; no phone calls and we definitely couldn't be seen together. Maybe he didn't even know. How long would I be stuck there? Lucas was no dummy. He had to have gone back for his keys; he would have found the broken coffee pot and my blood too. I looked down at my arm and ran my fingers over the gauze tightly wrapped around my stitches. Maybe Lamb had cleaned everything up and there wasn't any evidence at all that there had been a struggle.

I sighed heavily and walked over to the open window, tipping my chin up to let the breeze cool my face. I had to keep thinking positively. Maybe he'd tried to call or text and got nervous that I wasn't answering. Maybe he'd speak to my doorman; find out that no-one had seen me leave. I obviously couldn't count on my father to get me out of there, so without Lucas I was pretty much screwed.

The sound of the door opening behind me made me jump. I turned around to see Lamb and behind him walked in a tall, very muscular man. Holy shit…Vance Wallace.

"Hey, glad to see you're up and around." I crossed my arms and gave him a 'fuck you' look.

"Whoa…still angry I see," he said, holding his palms up in retreat. He dropped his hands and looked down at his shoes. "This is Vance Wallace. He came a long way to talk to you, Jen."

"Well, finally…the infamous Jennifer Callahan. Boy, have I been hearing a lot about you lately." Wallace crossed his arms and rubbed his chin with one of his hands while he looked me down and back up again, taking his time. He smacked his lips as his dark eyes met mine.

"I can see now what all the fuss is about. Thomas wasn't kidding when he said you were tough but I think he left out just how fine you are. You'll fit in good in California. We'll get some color on those cheeks."

He tried to touch my face but I turned away before he could. I walked away from him and shot Lamb another dirty look as I passed him. I snuck a look at the door. It was closed. Dammit.

Without missing a beat Wallace continued. "So here's what's gonna happen. I'm here to collect my goods from the dock tonight and then tomorrow you and Thomas will fly back to California. Once I get…"

"I'm not going anywhere with anyone."

He paused briefly and then very calmly picked up the chair from behind the desk and carried it over to me. My heart started racing, my already pounding head throbbing more. He dropped the chair down with a loud bang, right at my feet.

"Sit down and shut the fuck up. When I want you to speak I'll let you know so."

I didn't move. Half of me was pissed off as hell and didn't want him telling me what to do. The other half of me was scared to death and frozen in place. With one hand he reached to his back and pulled out a gun and pointed it at me. With his other hand he grabbed a fistful of my hair and pulled my head back.

"You want me to make you?"

With a hitch in of breath I sat down.

"That's what I thought" He dropped his hand with the gun to his side, which allowed me to relax ever so slightly. I knew what Wallace was capable of and I had no doubt he would shoot me if it suited him. "Now, as I was sayin', you and Thomas will go back to California and run things together there. Thomas seems to think you two have something going so, whatever...I don't give a shit. As long as his work gets done I could care less who he fucks."

A shudder ran down my spine. My suspicion that Thomas was interested in me was right, but Jesus, he had certainly exaggerated things to Wallace.

"When I'm done here I'll head down to L.A. myself and then you and I can get acquainted." He was standing behind me and I flinched when he pulled my hair off my shoulder and caressed my cheek. I leaned away from his touch and pushed out my jaw. Keep it together Jen.

I looked over at Lamb, hoping he could make some sense of what was going on. Why was Wallace talking about me working for him? "Lamb...why are you doing this to me? I trusted you."

He looked down, shaking his head in shame. He met my eyes again. "Look honey, I did this to protect you. When you were in California, Thomas assumed you were there for work on your father's behalf. He thought you knew all about what your father and I did and our business with Mr. Wallace. He also said the two of you had a cozy dinner together and he gave me the impression that there was something serious happening between you two. I had a feeling that wasn't true, but I needed to make sure."

"So it wasn't my father who called Thomas—it was you?"

He ignored my question. "So when you got back to New York I ha…"

"You had someone follow me!"

"I had someone let me know what you did and who you were with once you were home. When I got the report that you were with Lucas Benjamin…well, I knew Thomas had misunderstood and you'd started something you never would've been able to finish. I thought through all of this a thousand ways, honey, I really did. But bringing you here was my only way of keeping you safe."

I laughed at the absurdity. "You have a really fucked up version of safe."

"If I hadn't brought you here, Thomas was gonna find you were with Lucas and - well, let's just say it wouldn't have been good for you."

"You mean I would have been killed."

"That's right…just like your sweetie's parents," said Wallace. "You should know what that feels like. Must be why you two hooked up."

What the hell is he talking about? I looked at Lamb with raised eyebrows. "So why bring me here then? Why all the theatrics? Why couldn't you just talk to me at my apartment instead of knocking me out and locking me up?" My voice echoed slightly in the vastness of the warehouse.

"Because I needed time. If I had told you that your father and I work for a major drug dealer and help him get drugs in and out of the city, you would have run right to your boyfriend."

My eyes were wide and I blinked several times as the reality of what Lamb had said soaked in. His trips to California…the files at the beach house…Wallace always being released; it all made sense now. Wallace had people all over the city working and scamming for him. And my father was one of them.

"But what do I have to do with any of it? Are you planning to shut me up to make sure I don't ruin the good thing you have going?"

"We want you to be a part of it with us. It makes sense now that you're older and have so much experience as a defense attorney. You'd be a perfect asset in California, Jen." Lamb believed his bullshit so completely that he actually sounded sincere.

"How could you ever think I would want to be a part of this, Lamb? How could you? After what he did to Lucas's parents! Oh my god. I can't believe you would actually think I wo…"

"That rat got what he deserved." Wallace's voice made me flinch. "Nobody fucks me over like that and gets away with it. I only wish I had stuck around to finish the job. In due time, though."

"But his parents…they didn't do a thing to you! They didn't deserve that!" I said, choking back the threat of tears.

"They raised a fucking rat for a son, so yeah, I'd say they did."

Clearly it was a waste of time talking to Wallace. Lamb, on the other hand, maybe it wasn't too late for him to help me. "Lamb…please…you don't have to do this. Just let me go…we can figure it all out."

He looked away from me and out the windows. "It's out of my hands now. I'm sorry."

My head was still feeling heavy and now the throbbing went up a notch. I leaned forward and put my elbows on my knees, rubbing my temples in an effort to clear my mind. I needed to think straight, figure out what I could do. My skin prickled as I went through my options. If I didn't agree to work for Vance Wallace I was sure he would kill me. But there was no way I could do that. That wasn't who I was and there was no way I would betray Lucas like that. Maybe I could fake it and agree just so I could get out. Maybe I could get away at the airport and find some…

My thoughts were interrupted by a loud knock at the door. Lamb opened it.

"What the hell are you doing here?"

I leaned to one side so I could see around Lamb. My heart skipped as I thought for a brief second that it might be Lucas. Oh…it was just my father.

"I came here to see my daughter. I shouldn't need an appointment. Let me in,"

"Yeah, let him in Lamb," Wallace said.

"Jennifer…are you okay?"

"Yeah, peachy."

"Welcome to the party," Wallace said. "I was just in the process of discussing a new job description for your daughter. Seems like now would be a good time to teach her the full extent of the family business, don't 'cha think?"

"This is madness. I want you to let her go. She has nothing to do with this."

I sat up. Why was he sticking up for me? I'd thought that he couldn't

149

care less. Wallace exploded with laughter.

"That's a good one Phil. You really are a dumb fuck, ya know that? First of all, this bitch ain't goin' nowhere. And second, she ain't walkin' outta here unless she's on my payroll."

"I would never work for you, you fucking asshole!"

"Whew, she's feisty. Mm mm mm…I like that. I like that a lot." He ran a finger from my cheek down to my chin. It chilled my blood to ice.

"Get your fucking hands off me," I yelled, turning my head away from him.

"She has your attitude. But it's not completely inflexible, is it Phil? See if you can change her mind. Or I'll change it for her - just like I changed yours."

"What's he talking about?" I was tired of being the only one who didn't know.

"Don't." My father's angry words came out through gritted teeth.

"No you don't. I don't know who you think you are but you work for me. I call the shots around here. I'm runnin' out of patience…I'm sick of this bullshit. What's it gonna be? Huh?"

Wallace took a few steps closer to my father and was gesturing with his gun as he yelled at him. He looked at me. He grabbed my hair and I let out a yelp. I saw a drip of sweat run down his temple. I fought the urge to vomit.

"Maybe your daughter needs some incentive," Wallace said, turning the gun on my father.

The next thing I knew the room exploded. I covered my ears and screamed. When I looked up I saw my father lying on the floor, holding his shoulder.

"Daddy!" I cried. "You shot him...I can't believe you shot him!"

Lucas

Phillip's car was parked in the lot. I slowed down to a jog and stopped behind it. I put my hands on my knees so I could catch my breath and noticed that the place looked empty. I ventured a look over the top of the car; I spotted a door and figured that must have been the one I heard Phillip use. I eased my way over, scanning my surroundings as I went. I wasn't sure I was headed in the right direction. I pulled the handle slowly, hearing it whine. Thankfully Phillip must have left it unlocked. I pulled my gun out of my waistband and took one last deep breath. I counted to three and swung the door open. With the quick force it barely made any noise, giving nothing away to whoever was inside. I closed it carefully.

It was humid and damp inside with a little daylight coming through the filthy windows. I walked to my right and stayed close to the side of the wall with my gun up and ready. There wasn't much inside. There were a few large crates randomly placed, a stairwell against the northern wall and a door ajar all the way in the back that looked like it led to an office. I saw light coming from the room and I figured I should go there next.

As I got closer to the office door I heard voices and shuffling.

"Leave him be! You're lucky I'm feeling gracious and didn't just kill him."

I squatted down against the wall and took a quick peek around the door frame. Phillip was lying on the ground clutching his left shoulder, his face twisted with pain. I looked again and, by some miracle Phillip saw me, then quickly looked back down.

Jennifer

I shot up so I could go to my father, but Wallace was even faster, and pushed hard against my shoulder, driving me back into the chair. The

151

front feet of the chair came up as my weight hit and I nearly tilted over backwards.

"Sit your ass back down."

"He's bleeding!"

"That was the point. Now sit there and shut up."

He walked over to the windows behind me, out of my sight. I looked over to my father; he had rolled onto his hip, clutching at his shoulder. Behind him I saw the office door was open. I could make it...I know I could. My eyes flicked back to my father and immediately I changed my mind. If I ran out of there, Wallace would either shoot me in the back, or kill my father. I was so helpless I couldn't stand it. I was sick to my stomach, a vile mix of anger and fear coiling through my gut. My emotions had been pushed to the extreme and I didn't know how much more I could tolerate.

Lamb went over to my father and knelt down.

"You okay?" he asked softly, remorse in his voice.

Wallace walked over to my father, briefly pointing the gun at him again. Then he walked over to me.

"Now, let's get back to business. What's it gonna be missy? Your daddy here is waiting for an answer."

I was overwhelmed. I needed time to think; time to work out some kind of idea to keep both myself and my father alive. I pinched the bridge of my nose and closed my eyes, trying to calm down.

"Jennifer, please," Lamb said walking back behind me. "You can end this right now. I promise I won't let anything happen to you,"

All the images of him masquerading as some kind of protector, some kind of father figure seemed phony to me now. I wanted to tell him all the things I was thinking of him but I knew it wasn't the time or place. Suddenly, I saw movement. My father was up and running across the room. He tackled Lamb.

Lucas

Phillip looked out at me again and I mouthed the word Jen to him. He nodded, which I took as confirmation she was okay. Thank God. He was looking at me with wide eyes.

"Jennifer, please, you can end this right now. I promise I won't let anything happen to you."

I heard Lamb's voice coming from the back of the room, closest to where Phillip was. Phillip was back looking at me again, flicking his head to his left. I nodded. I wasn't sure what I was about to do but I had to trust my instincts. Could I do this? What if something went wrong and Jen got hurt? I'd never forgive myself. In a blink Phillip was up and darting out of my view. I stood up with my back against the wall, my heart pounding out of my chest. Now or never. I slid one step to my right and turned to see chaos in the room. Phillip and Lamb were tangled up in the back of the room fighting dangerously close to the enormous floor to ceiling windows. One of the large windows was slightly open, bringing in the ocean air coming up the cliff outside. Wallace was pointing a gun in the direction of the two men fighting, confusion on his face. Jen was sitting in a chair in the middle of the room.

"Freeze," I said, my voice echoing behind me.

"Lucas!" Jen cried.

"What the…" Wallace turned his gun onto me.

"Put down your gun."

"Oh, this?" Wallace said, waving his gun around. "You don't like it pointed at you, huh? Well maybe it would be better pointed at your little girlfriend here, how 'bout that?"

Jennifer

Wallace had his gun up against my temple and I froze. My eyes stung as tears welled up. I looked back to see Lamb stumbling, trying to catch his footing. He grasped at the side of the window, scrambling to catch himself, but lost his grip. He fell back against the large window, which pushed it open further. With wide eyes, Lamb began to fall, but he managed to grab the windowsill. My father tried to grab for him but it was too late – Lamb's fingers slipped and he disappeared. I couldn't believe it - Lamb was surely dead. I covered my face with my hands and sobbed. The moment was quickly over when I heard Vance Wallace's voice.

"Put your gun down Josh. Oh sorry, I mean Lucas. You dirty fucking rat. I should have just shot you that night at your parents' house. I thought for sure when the ceiling caved in you were dead. I plan to make sure I finish it completely tonight though."

Lucas looked blank for a moment and then anger erupted in his eyes.

Lucas

The flash of the last nightmare I had had came rushing back to me. Wallace was pointing a gun at me…I was standing in my parents' living room; it was engulfed in flames…the ceiling collapsed and knocked me out. I remembered. I remembered everything. Holy hell, Wallace was there and he was gonna kill me too.

"You son of a bitch,"

Wallace laughed low and throaty. "Drop that fucking gun or I'll kill her too."

I looked at Jen. Her face was ashen and her bottom lip was quivering. A tear rolled down her cheek and the fear in her eyes shattered my heart. I dropped my arm to my side and tossed the gun to my right.

Phillip staggered over, the front of his suit covered in blood. His nose was bleeding too. "Let her go."

I could hear the echo of sirens coming in through the window. I imagined Sarge was outside, back up in full force. I wasn't sure how much time there was before Wallace started shooting all of us, but I had to do something to get the gun pointed away from Jen.

I took a step towards Wallace and sure enough, it worked. He pointed the gun right at me. "Don't fucking move."

I put my hands up, letting him know he was in charge. Jen was shaking. My body ached at the compulsion to hold her. "It's okay hon… it's gonna be okay."

"Fuck this. Time's up, so say bye bye to your boyfriend. See you in hell Lucas."

In a flash I heard the gun go off and immediately I ducked to my right, praying like hell the bullet had missed me, or at the very least hadn't hit any vital organs. I landed on the floor and saw Phillip jump up then fall next to me. My gun was inches away from me. Jen jumped up and attacked Wallace with a barrage of punches to his face and chest. He dropped his gun. "You stupid fucking bitch." He back-handed her in the face. She slumped to the ground with a moan. Fury fired up in me like a volcano about to burst. I grabbed my gun and rolled onto my back, seeing Wallace at the same time about to point his gun at me. I fired over and over and over until I heard nothing but a click every time I pulled the trigger.

Jennifer

My ears cleared and I could hear lots of noise in the room. I lifted my head and found the room wasn't spinning any more. Finally my eyes focused on Lucas. He was looking at me, asking if I was okay.

"Lucas! Oh Lucas, I'm so sorry!"

"Hey, everything's fine now. It's over."

I put my hands on his face, making sure what I was seeing was real.

"We're gonna need a medic!"

I didn't recognize the voice but I turned to look. A man wearing a bullet proof vest was kneeling over my father. I ran over to him and knelt at his head. "Oh my God, Daddy! Don't move…the ambulance is coming so you're gonna be just fine." I started stroking his hair, trying not to look at the blood pooling next to him. I knew it was bad. I felt Lucas come up beside me and start rubbing my back.

"Jennifer…" my father said. Trying to speak made him choke and I could hear how hard it was for him to breathe. Seeing him in pain and pleading with me was gut-wrenching. The icy wall of anger I had built was now shattered and gone.

"Stop talking Daddy, just sit still." I wanted him to shut up.

"No, I need to tell you…I love you with all my heart…your mother loved you…I'm sorry…I wasn't the father…that you deserved."

"Stop that Daddy. You did the best you could. I love you too. Now shut up and be still."

"It was…never your fault. I was trying…to protect you…I'm so sorry…"

"I know Daddy, I know." I had no idea what he was talking about but it was tearing my heart into pieces. My stone-faced, overbearing, imperious father was pouring his heart out to me and it was breaking my soul.

"Lucas…please take care of her…"

"I will sir."

My father took a big breath in and let it out with a whistle from his chest. His head fell to the side and he didn't move again. "Daddy!" I screamed at him, trying to shake him back to life. He couldn't be dead. No. He was just resting. He just needed to take a break. He was talking too much so he just needed to rest a minute.

"In here!"

Men circled around him. Finally…someone to help.

"Ma'am, you need to step aside please."

I looked up. What? What did he say? I looked down at my father and his eyes were wide open; blank and vacant. Oh my God…he was dead. Reality was seeping in. Lucas pulled me up but my legs couldn't hold me. I crashed into him and broke down.

"He's gone."

I turned and looked back at my father. His eyes were closed. He was still and quiet. He was dead. It was real; what I already knew, confirmed. I put my head into Lucas's chest. I was completely broken.

Lucas picked me up into his arms and started walking. I didn't care where he was taking me because I knew I was safe with him. He had saved my life and rescued me from Vance Wallace…the man who had killed his parents…and the man who had killed my father.

Lucas

We walked into utter chaos. Police vehicles, ambulances, fire trucks, media vans, people everywhere.

"Lucas!"

I turned around and saw Sarge.

"I need your car," I said.

He paused. I knew he needed my statement and also wanted to give me hell for going against his direction. But he knew I needed to get Jen out of there. "The keys are in it…over there." He gestured with his chin in the direction of a Grand Marquis at the edge of the lot.

"Thanks…I owe you."

The media were swarmed like angry bees buzzing behind the yellow police tape. A couple of officers were standing close by to keep them at bay. I slipped Jen into the car and slid her over to the passenger side. She was limp and laid her head in my lap with her hands clutching my leg, sobs still trembling through her body. I stroked her hair and drove slowly away from the warehouse.

Part 4

Jennifer

Chapter Twenty

I awoke feeling too hot. I was lying in a bed; comfortable but way too warm. The feel of Lucas curled up behind me explained the heat. I stirred, making his head shoot up.

"Hey…are you okay?"

"Yeah I'm fine. I just need to pee."

He removed his arm that was draped over my waist and I pushed myself up. Ugh! I moaned at the feel of my sore body and pounding head. Lucas jumped up out of bed and was instantly at my side.

"Here, let me help you."

I used his forearm to brace myself and attempted to stand. My legs were shaky, but I was able to find my balance. I took a small step and didn't crumble into a heap. That was a good start.

Lucas helped me into the bathroom of his new apartment. It was the first time I had been there and from what little I saw of it, he hadn't done much unpacking. There were boxes against the walls of the bedroom. There was just his bed and a dresser, making the space feel enormous. It was double the size of his old apartment and the cool hardwood floors felt good under my feet.

He leaned me against the counter and flicked a switch. I braced myself for too much light but was pleasantly surprised to see a soft glow appear above the shower and nowhere else.

"You think you can handle it from here?" he said, bending his knees to be level with me.

"I think so."

"I'll go make some coffee. I'll leave the door open a little so if you need me just call, okay?"

"Okay. Thank you Lucas." I could feel the tears start to burn behind my eyes. Lack of sleep mixed with being an emotional mess - any little thing set me off. I leaned my forehead into his chest, not wanting him to worry.

He took my shoulders lightly and kissed my hair.

"I'll be right back." He padded out and left the door ajar.

I thought about everything that had happened after Lucas took me out of the warehouse and to the hospital. The wave of nurses, doctors, tests, and X-rays happened in a blurry haze. I had attempted to give a statement to Sergeant Brentzel but my mind was fuzzy, half from the pain killers, half from still being in shock. I was glad Lucas had brought me back to his place.

With my palms bracing me on the counter behind, I pushed myself forward and was feeling more stable. I turned around and was shocked by my reflection in the mirror. I leaned over and flicked a switch, making the lights above the mirror come on. I winced briefly and my mouth came open as the stranger in the mirror did the same thing.

My long hair was a tangled, knotted mess. Bedhead would have been a gentle term. My left cheek was an array of dark colors, showing the swollen evidence of Vance Wallace's punishment. Dark circles had formed under my listless green eyes and my lips were dry and cracked. I reached up and touched my cheek with one fingertip, still unable to believe it was real. The small cut on my cheekbone burned when I touched it. Ow, dammit. My forearm was newly bandaged and the pounding in my head made my ears ring.

I braced my way down the counter to the toilet. I went back to the sink and was desperate to brush my teeth and hair. I needed to find some semblance of my old self and to hide as much evidence as possible of what happened. I was rummaging through drawers when Lucas came in.

"Hey…what are you looking for?" he asked, placing a cup of coffee on the counter for me. The smell was glorious.

I sighed and leaned my butt against the counter, not wanting to see the monster of my reflection anymore. I picked up the coffee and took a sip. "I look terrible."

He pulled open a drawer and closed it. He took my elbow and said, "Come on". He led me back to the bed. "Sit."

I crawled onto the bed and sat cross legged with my hands wrapped around the mug. I felt the pressure of him sitting behind me and he put his hands on my shoulders. "Sit still."

Gently, he started brushing my hair. He took his time, working through the knots and tangles with expert ease. He was careful not to pull when he hit a knot and made sure it was broken before pulling the brush through.

I softened at the tender way he was caring for me. The time I had spent in the warehouse felt like a week's worth of hell even though it had only been twenty-four hours. My will had been tested and my emotions were raw. I wasn't sure what to think or how to feel about anything anymore. The only thing I didn't question was Lucas and the fact that he had saved my life.

I was spent. Fried. Beat down and broken both inside and out. I closed my eyes and a brief moment of reality snuck in. My father was dead. Lamb was dead. Vance Wallace was dead. My life was never going to be the same again and I couldn't sift through it all to decide whether to be glad or worried.

Lucas picked up on my tension.

"What are you thinking? Talk to me."

I sighed and took a sip of coffee, stalling so I could choose which thought to bring up first. "I've been thinking a lot about my father and what he was saying right before...right before he died." Saying those words out loud was making the reality that much more real. "I wish I understood. I have so many questions. And now I'll never know."

"What kind of questions?"

"I don't know...like saying it wasn't my fault and he was trying to protect me. I mean, I guess I could assume he was talking about Lamb taking me and how my father didn't do anything to get me out. Maybe he was just delirious." I pushed back the memory of him being in pain and dying. It was too hard. With a shrug of a shoulder I continued. "I can't think of anything else he would mean."

Lucas finished brushing my hair and took my coffee mug. He sat back against the headboard and pulled me to lie against his chest. I eased into his embrace and knotted my fingers with his.

"Your father loved you very much. All he wanted was for you to be safe."

"I wish you could've met him properly. I really think he would've liked you a lot."

We sat in silence for a long moment. "I actually did get a chance to know him."

I sat up and turned to face him. "What do you mean? When?"

"Sarge and I were working with him while you were in the warehouse. The last two times he was there he was wearing a wire and I heard every word."

So, in a way, Lucas had been there. He had been my angel waiting in the wings for the right time to come and get me. And in the end he had. It made me angry my father had waited until the last minute to finally buck up and want to do the right thing. It pissed me off that he had said everything at the last minute; all the things I had been waiting to hear since my mother had died. And now he was dead and I was never going to get the chance to tell him that I was sorry. Sorry for being difficult and making him hate me.

"I'm just glad he brought you to me. I wouldn't be here if it weren't for you. You saved my life, Lucas. Vance Wallace would have killed me if you hadn't come in when..." My voice broke off and I swallowed past the lump that had formed in my throat.

"Shhh," he said rubbing my good cheek with the back of his knuckles. "It wasn't just me, you know. Your father took the bullet meant for me. He was the bigger hero, if you ask me."

I wasn't sure I understood what he meant. I thought back and wondered if I was remembering it differently. Lucas must have seen my confusion.

"Wallace meant to shoot and kill me. Your father jumped in the way and blocked the bullet."

I leaned into his chest and pressed my forehead into his neck. I cried softly for my father, this time with a new respect.

"There are some things you don't know; things I think you should know. After what happened to me and going around not remembering anything...well, it's not a good feeling." He wrapped his arms around me. "Your father wasn't the man you think he was, hon. He did everything he did because he was trying to protect you and keep you safe."

I sat up and met his eyes. "What are you talking about?"

He pushed a hand through his hair and sucked in a breath of air. "Vance Wallace killed your mom. He killed her because she knew too much and your father wanted out of the business."

I scrambled off the bed. "No, no, no...you have it all wrong. My mother died in a car accident - key word being accident. No one killed her! Why would you say such a thing?"

He sat up and put his feet on the floor. "Because your father told me."

I took a step back away from him. "He would say anything to save his own ass and make himself look good. He was never around and shipped me off the first chance he got." I began pacing a distressed circle around the room. "I can't believe he used my mother's death to excuse him from having to be a father."

"That's not how it was Jen...not it at all. Think about it - think about what Wallace said to your father about changing your mind...just like Wallace had changed his. Your mom found out what your dad was up to with Wallace and the drugs. She threatened to leave him if he didn't get out. Wallace wasn't the kind of man you just walked away from, especially when your father had become such an important asset."

I stopped pacing and faced him.

"You were in the car with your mom when it crashed. Once your mom was killed your father had one thing left - you. And he was going to do everything necessary to keep you safe and away from danger. Don't you see - your dad was the danger. In his eyes, he was putting you in jeopardy by working for Wallace."

I thought back to all the cryptic shit everybody understood except me. Oh my God - my mother, my poor mother. Could it be true? Was he right? Lucas would never lie to me. The dream I always had; the one where my mom was driving and looking back at me. Had that actually happened?

Lucas came to me and took my shoulders. "He loved you Jen. And he thought the best way to love you would be to send you as far away from him as possible. Put yourself in your father's shoes - would you have done any different?"

I looked at him as tears streaked down my cheeks. He cupped my face and wiped them away with his thumbs.

"He was afraid to get close to you. He couldn't risk Wallace doing to you what he had done to your mother. And I get that - I know exactly how that feels. Every time you were away from me and I couldn't be around to protect you I was scared to death. I failed trying to keep my parents safe. While you were in that warehouse - I've never felt more helpless. Your father wasn't as selfish as I was though. He gave you up in order to keep you alive. He made the ultimate sacrifice; he had just lost his wife and had to lose his daughter all at the same time. And in the end he not only saved your life, he saved mine as well."

My knees gave out. Lucas caught me and we sank to the ground together. He pulled me into his lap and rubbed up and down my back. I was boneless. I felt wrung out and empty. My father had been through years of letting me think he hated me and never told me the truth. All he had had to do was tell me what had really happened and I would've understood all of it. But he chose to keep it from me thinking he was protecting me. I used to think I was smart and could read people well. I never read what was really going on with my father because I was so caught up with how I felt. I never gave him the benefit of the doubt. And now he was gone.

Lucas stood up and took me to bed. He climbed in behind me and pulled me close against him. He held me tight and didn't say anything more. He let me cry until exhaustion took over and I fell asleep.

Chapter Twenty-one

I opened my eyes when I heard the phone ring. I didn't know what time it was, what day it was or how long I had been sleeping. I rolled onto my back and looked at the ceiling while I took an inventory of how I felt. My head hurt but it had moved from mind bending throbs down to a dull roar. My cheek felt swollen and my arm itched from the stitches.

I sat up and put my feet on the cool floor. Where was Lucas? I stood up and made my way to the bathroom, ignoring the mirror. When I'd finished I padded down a short hallway and into the living room and recognized the furniture. Somehow it fit better in his new place. There were narrow floor to ceiling windows that allowed spectacular natural light into the room. It glowed so bright and cheery that it put a smile on my face. A cool breeze from an open window blew across my face. I could hear light traffic coming up from the street. People were laughing, and my mood was improving by the second.

I heard some noise coming from another room. I followed the sounds until I arrived at a second bedroom that Lucas had turned into what looked like an office. There was a small wooden desk and a leather office chair behind it with a panoramic view of the city coming through the windows. Lucas was talking on the phone, leaning his hip against a window. He was wearing worn jeans that hung just at his hips and no shirt. His feet were bare and his hair looked damp, probably fresh from a shower. His shoulder flexed as he ran a hand through his hair. His face had a few days' worth of stubble and for a moment I took in the awesome view of the man I loved. I had thought so much of Lucas in the time I was alone in the warehouse but nothing could compare to the real thing. As I took a step into the room, the floor creaked, giving me away. He turned and his face lit up.

"Lemme call you back." He strode the distance between us and embraced me tightly. His clean smell and bare skin ignited my body. I ran my hands down his back and put them in his back pockets. I had to slow down because I knew I didn't have a drop of energy to do what my body wanted to.

"How you feeling?" he asked, pulling me back by my shoulders.

With a shrug of a shoulder I said, "I'm alright I guess. What time is it?"

"It's almost noon. You hungry?"

"Starved!"

He put his arm around my shoulders and led me to the kitchen. He sat me down in a chair at the island and pulled out a cutting board, then went to the refrigerator.

"Your new place is really nice. I like it here a lot," I said, leaning on the cool marble with my chin in my hands. Watching him move around the kitchen felt normal and natural. Someone from the outside looking in would never guess what we had just survived. I bet the way I looked would give it away. I sat up feeling suddenly self-conscious. I pulled at my hair and Lucas laughed.

"You look fine, stop fidgeting."

"Easy for you to say. You look like a God. I look like I just got my ass kicked and haven't showered for two days. Oh wait - that's exactly what happened."

"So go take a shower," he said casually, while slicing a tomato.

The idea sounded like heaven.

"I had Roxanne bring over some of your stuff. There's a bag in my room next to the dresser," he said, gesturing with the knife in the direction of the bedroom.

"Roxanne was here?" I asked with a twinge of guilt. "She must be royally pissed at me."

"No she's not...stop. She was worried about you. She heard about what happened on the news and came to the hospital. You were sleeping though, so she never got to see you."

"I bet she gave you the third degree."

He laughed. "Well, let's just say she wasn't all that thrilled you had been keeping me a secret. She understood why after I explained a few things." He finished with the tomatoes and started slicing cucumbers. "Roxanne is really great. I like her a lot."

"Well, don't like her too much." I surprised myself at the jealousy I was feeling. How stupid it was for me to think Lucas would have a thing for Roxanne. But the way I looked at the moment wasn't helping matters.

Twisted Memories

Lucas stopped his cutting and came around the island to me. He spun me around in my seat so I was facing him and he braced his hands on the counter, making a cage around me. "I know you've been through hell and back the past couple of days which is why I'm giving you a pass on what you just said. But I don't ever want you to doubt how much you mean to me. I love you more than just saying those words could ever mean. You're everything to me."

I was ashamed of myself. It had been a hard couple of days and Lucas was the only good thing that had come out of it all. He was all I had left and the last thing I wanted was to sabotage anything with him. "I love you too," I said, wrapping my arms around his waist. He put his arms around me and pulled me closer to him. "You're right. I'm sorry."

"Why don't you go take a shower while I finish up making lunch?"

I stood up and kissed his lips softly. He patted my rear lightly, a playful smile on his face. "Be back in a bit," I said and went back to the bedroom.

I opened the bag Roxanne had brought and found all of my usual bathroom items, underwear, bra, a pair of jeans and a t-shirt. There was my brush and hairdryer. Also, inside a small, black velvet bag was a bottle of my favorite perfume. I loved how well Roxanne knew me.

I took the bag and all its contents to the bathroom and turned on the light over the shower. I turned the water on hot, undressed, putting all of my clothes in a pile to throw out. I didn't plan on wearing any of the things that would remind me of the past couple of days.

I adjusted the water and stepped in. It was hot and took me a moment to get used to it but it felt oh so good. I wished it would burn the top layer of my skin off to remove all the touches, punishments, dirt and ugliness. I put my head back and let the water wet my hair. It ran in thick streams down my face and I cringed when it crossed over the cut on my cheek. I ran my hands over my hair and I felt the bandage on my arm getting heavy. I pulled the tape off and unraveled the thick gauze and dropped it on the tile floor of the bathroom. I needed to feel the pain. I needed it to remind me that I was still strong and could handle anything.

My body was bruised and scarred but it would heal. Eventually I would look just like I always had and whoever saw me wouldn't see any evidence of the hurt. Knowing my mother had been murdered was fresh pain. I was mourning her all over again, almost as if it had just happened. My father had been murdered by the same man but I wasn't going to let it break me. I couldn't.

I finished up with my shower. I felt rejuvenated. I had gone from battered to bold. Funny what a shower could do. After dressing and drying my hair, the smell from the kitchen was making my stomach grumble. I found Lucas setting the island with plates full of steaming pasta. There was a small salad next to each plate and I grinned at him

"This looks amazing."

"Sit. Eat. Enjoy."

"I didn't know you could cook." I sniffed at the steam. "What is this?"

"It's tortellini with a basil sauce. I figured you could use some carbs," he said, taking a big bite.

"This is delicious. If I had known you could cook like this I would have suggested we stay in more often."

He smiled. "How was your shower? Did you find everything you needed?"

"Yeah, the shower felt great. I'm going to have to call Roxanne. I'm sure she's got all kinds of questions."

"Speaking of calls," he said, wiping his mouth, "your father's lawyer called my cell looking for you."

My heart sank. "What did he want?"

"He wants to go over your father's estate with you. He said it couldn't wait."

"What the hell? For Christ's sake it's been what…twenty-four hours?"

"Look at it this way - the sooner you talk to him, the quicker you can move on."

I realized Lucas was right. Maybe it was best to get all the practical stuff taken care of. "I'll call him after I eat."

After a few moments of silence I was feeling more at ease. Lucas finished and took his dishes to the sink. "So what happens now?" I asked.

He turned around and leaned on the counter in front of me. "What happens now with what?"

I wasn't really sure what I meant. I mindlessly began pushing a tortellini around on my plate. "I guess with me. And with my work. And maybe with us." I kept my gaze on my plate.

"Well…" he began. "What is it that you want, Jen? Do you want to continue working at your father's firm? Take over the business and all that?"

"No, I don't. It would be hard never knowing if I was putting criminals back on the streets so they could hurt people over and over. I just couldn't do it." I shook my head trying to get the image of Vance Wallace out of my mind.

"Then that answers that question." He reached across the island and took one of my hands. "What happens now with us is easy." I looked up and my eyes met his. "I love you, Jennifer, and now we can just be us. We can be the 'us' we wanted to be from the moment we first met. There's nothing keeping us apart any more. I don't think I could stand to be apart from you for another minute."

I smiled. It was exactly what I wanted to hear; what I needed to hear. Lucas was my life now.

"And lastly," He let go of my hand and stood back up. "What happens with you is anything you want." He shrugged a shoulder. "You control your life. There's nothing to worry about or hold you back anymore." He stood rinsing the dishes at the sink with his back to me. I watched his muscles flex while he worked. I licked my bottom lip. I needed to be closer to him. I stood up, walked around the island and leaned on it right behind him.

"What about you?" I asked.

He turned the water off and spun around. He leaned against the sink facing me, wiping his hands on a dish towel. "Well, now that I have my memory back, Sarge wants me to talk with the department shrink again. He thinks it's time for me to get my shield back."

Not all that surprised by his answer, I smiled. I knew how much he had missed his work as a detective. "And what do you think?"

He flipped the dish towel over my head and locked it behind my back. He pulled slightly until I was flush against him and I braced myself with my palms on his chest. Being close to him was making all of my senses react. He smelled clean and fresh from a shower. The feel of his warm skin sent a shiver up my arms. The look on his face had become serious as his hooded eyes met mine. He kissed me softly on the lips and I could taste basil. "You are so beautiful," he said, curling his fingers around the back of my neck. The sound of his words made my knees weak.

"Right now, this is all I want to think about." He leaned in and kissed me deeply. I kissed him back, pushing my hands through his hair. After a moment he pulled back, leaving me breathless. He ran the backs of his knuckles down my cheek and neck. He traced a line across my collarbone and shoulder, down my side, letting his thumb run over my erect nipple. I closed my eyes and welcomed the way it felt when he touched me. My body was exploding with need and desire and I wasn't going to hold back from it one bit. Not anymore.

"I want you to make love to me, Lucas," I whispered.

He didn't say a word, but picked me up and held me close against him. He kissed me softly and carried me to the bedroom.

Chapter Twenty-two

Lucas and I had spent most of the afternoon in bed. When I couldn't avoid it any more, I got up and spoke to my father's lawyer. Without hearing anything more than "It's urgent" as an explanation, Lucas and I left as soon as possible to meet him.

It was dusk and Lucas switched on his headlights as we hit the 495 to Long Island. Jacob Brach had been my father's lawyer ever since I could remember. When I was young, my parents had taken me to his house for parties and weekend barbecues, but I hadn't been to Long Island since then. Those were good memories; the kind I planned to think about more often.

It was just after six o'clock when Lucas pulled into the long driveway. He got out, walked around to my side and opened the door. He held out his hand. "You ready?"

I accepted his hand and twined my fingers with his. I squeezed tight as we walked to the front door. "It's gonna be okay, don't worry."

I rang the doorbell and was greeted moments later by a woman wearing a black and white maid's uniform. "Good evening" said the maid. "Mr. Brach is expecting you. Please, come in and follow me." We followed the maid down a long hallway and paused while she opened a huge door at the end. She stepped aside. We went in and I heard the door close softly behind us.

Brach stood up from behind his desk and came around to greet us.

"Jennifer…so glad you came." He opened his arms as he approached me, pulling me into a tight embrace. "I'm so sorry."

"Whatever is going on must be pretty important for you to need to see me on a Sunday."

"It is. Please, come in and sit down."

We walked to his desk and, before sitting down, Jacob looked at Lucas. "I'm sorry…I didn't get your name."

"Forgive me Jacob. This is Lucas Benjamin. He was working the Vance Wallace case and now…well, now he's my boyfriend." I felt my cheeks heat from embarrassment. It was awkward revealing my personal life to someone who was practically a stranger to me.

"Ah, Mr. Benjamin, it's nice to finally meet you. Phillip spoke highly of you. Thank you for coming with Jennifer today. She could certainly use the support."

"I have to say, we're both a bit anxious."

Jacob turned to me. "I spoke to your father the night he died. It was right before he left to go to the police station. He left explicit instructions that if anything were to happen to him that night that I was to meet with you right away and give you this." He picked up a white envelope and handed it to me.

"What's in it?" I asked. My hand shook as I took the envelope.

"I don't know. But he was very adamant about you getting it."

I looked at Lucas, butterflies in my stomach. He must have seen it in my eyes because he reached over and took my hand. I looked down at the plain white envelope in my lap and couldn't believe that such a small thing could hold so much power. But it did. I wasn't sure if I could handle any more stress. Watching my father die and learning my mother had been murdered had taken me to the brink.

"While you're here," Jacob said, interrupting my whirling thoughts, "I'll go over Phillip's will with you as well."

❧

An hour later, Lucas and I were back in the car driving down I 495. My head was spinning. I hadn't paid much attention as Jacob had gone over all the things I would inherit from my father. I just didn't care. I clutched the envelope in my hands, feeling its soft, smooth surface in between my fingers.

"Hey, you alright?" I felt Lucas's hand grip my leg. "You haven't said anything since we left. Tell me what you're thinking."

I sighed and my shoulders sagged. "This thing feels like a thousand pound weight in my lap right now."

"I can imagine. Whatever your dad wrote must be pretty important. He went through a lot of trouble to make sure you didn't wait to read it."

"But what could possibly be so important? Do you think it's about my mother?"

"You'll never know what it says until you read it."

I knew he was right. Dammit. Damn Vance Wallace. Damn my father. Damn this stupid letter.

Twisted Memories

そのめ

It was midnight and I was sitting at the office desk in Lucas's apartment. The letter sat staring at me from the blotter as I stared back like it was a ticking time bomb. I sipped my glass of Jack Daniels, waiting for it to kick in and give me some courage. I took a deep breath and downed the last of the whiskey. "Now or never," I said as I picked up a letter opener.

My hands were clammy and shaking as I placed the tip of the letter opener at a corner of the envelope. I sliced open the top with a quick rip and pulled out the contents. Two sheets of neatly folded paper were inside. I slowly unfolded them and saw my father's neat cursive handwriting. My eyes filled with tears at the sight. I sniffed and wiped my face with the back of my hand. I could do this. I pressed the paper flat and began reading.

Dear Jennifer,

If you are reading this letter, it means that something didn't go as planned and I am dead. But I don't want you to think about that. As hard as that may be for you to do, you'll understand why.

There are some things that you should know. Things that I've kept from you and for reasons you may not understand. I've always loved you Jennifer - more than I ever expressed - and it's time for you to know the whole truth.

God, I loved your mother. When I first met her at a charity function she was the only light in the room. And the fact she wanted to have anything to do with me not only shocked the hell out of me but scared me as well. She was so young and beautiful. I wondered why she would ever want an old man like me. But we fell in love and it no longer mattered. When she told me she was pregnant with you I was thrilled. The idea of having a child consumed me and it changed my life. You were so small and fragile when you were born. You looked into my eyes and I thought nothing would ever make my life better.

The three of us were perfect. Life was perfect. Or so I thought. My first mistake was taking Vance Wallace as a client. My second mistake was allowing myself to be threatened into working for him. My mistakes piled up one after the other and nothing was ever the same again.

When your mother had her car accident, it wasn't an accident at all. A man who worked for Wallace ran her off the road, causing her to go down an embankment. When I got to the hospital, you were safe, thank God, but I found out it was too late for her. But it wasn't too late for the child she was carrying.

For two long, excruciating months, your mother was kept alive on life support so the child could fully develop. They delivered the child - a girl - on July 19th. Your mother died the same day. You see Jennifer - you have a sister. Her name is Gabriella and she will be twenty-one this year. She lives in California with Manny and Gloria Fiori.

Your mother's death devastated me. And the fact that it was my fault is something I've lived with every day since. It was extremely difficult keeping the fact that the baby had survived a secret. I couldn't let Vance Wallace know about her. You and your sister were the only things I had left and I was going to do whatever I could to keep you both safe. I spent a few hours with Gabriella after she was born. It was arranged a month prior to her birth that Manny and his wife would take her. They were unable to have children of their own and I knew she would be safe with them. The next thing I had to do was send you away. That was even harder than letting your sister go. You were my princess and I loved you more than life itself. But I just couldn't risk you becoming a pawn, an object that Vance Wallace saw as leverage to keep me working for him. He killed your mother because I wanted to leave his business. There was no way I was going to risk that fate for you or your sister. I was weak and stupid. I should have tried harder instead of giving in to everyone's threats. But I was also scared. I felt as if I had no other choice.

I hope that one day you will find a way to forgive me for all of this. As hard as these past years have been, I would have done the same things again because it's what kept you safe. Having you work with me has allowed me to see the wonderful and beautiful woman you grew into. You look so much like your mother but you got your natural talent as a lawyer from me. I'm so proud of you Jennifer. You've become an amazing person and I've considered myself a very lucky man to have been able to see it firsthand. I wanted so badly to be close to you but the risks were too high. When George took you I knew there was nothing left to salvage of my life. All that matters is you. I will get you out of there, I promise you.

Twisted Memories

Lucas is a good man. It was meant to be for the two of you. I know he will care for you in all the ways that I never did. I have comfort in that.

As for your sister - go to her. Tell her everything. Manny knew there was always a possibility this would happen. But the two of you need each other. All the proof she is my daughter will be with my lawyer. Tell her about me Jennifer. I want the lies to be over once and for all.

All my love
Dad

Chapter Twenty-three

Three months later

We'd been at the beach house for almost a week. We'd planned a two week getaway, because when we got back to the city our lives were going to be completely different.

I sat in a lounge chair on the back deck, still reading through the box of my mother's journals, one propped up on my bent knees. A seagull squawked overhead so I looked up and shaded my eyes with one of my hands. I saw Lucas off in the distance, jogging down the beach.

I had been in a state of denial for a while after meeting with Jacob Brach and reading the letter my father left me. We'd gone back to see Jacob for the proof that I had a sister. He had it, in black and white, the birth certificate of one Gabriella Marie Monroe. A DNA test confirmed paternity.

But now time was moving more slowly. My father had left me everything; his penthouse apartment in Manhattan, the beach house, his business. I had put half of everything in a trust for Gabriella, hoping one day to meet her so she could have her rightful share. Then there was Lamb's will. With no wife or family to speak of, he had named me the sole beneficiary. I felt sure it was his way of paying me back for the role he played in my mothers' death. That was the kind of man he had been. He had never been anything but loving and kind to me. I could only guess that he worked for a man like Vance Wallace because it made him feel important.

With the two estates together I had more money than I knew what to do with, and I didn't want it. The first thing I did was sell my stock in the law firm. With no desire to work there, I wanted to sever all ties.

I wanted none of the money Lamb had left me. He had saved over two million dollars working for Wallace. Drug money. Shame money. I decided to give it away. I chose three different charities and set aside an amount for the police station. Sergeant Brentzel was happy to have the extra funds to update equipment.

I moved out of my apartment and in with Lucas. We had known each other for only a couple of months, and had the situation been different, there would've been no way I'd moved in with a man that soon. But Lucas and I had been through so much, it was an easy decision to make.

My father was laid to rest on a rainy Tuesday. I spent the remainder of that week going back and forth to his penthouse, clearing things out, deciding what to keep and what to get rid of before the sale was finalized. It was a grueling and extremely difficult process. Afterwards, I hibernated with Lucas at his apartment for weeks.

It took many trips back and forth to the station for Lucas to receive his reinstatement as detective. Whenever he was out I moped around, trying to figure out what to do with my future. I had no family, no career and enough money to live off of for the rest of my life. One day Lucas came home from the station and triggered the idea for my new career move.

"So the guys are all sitting around, waiting to hear back from ADA Donati," Lucas explained, leaning against the counter with his feet crossed at his ankles while I sat at the island with a cup of tea. "Meanwhile, the perp, who is being tailed, is going all over the city doing his usual business and no one can touch him without that warrant. It was the biggest waste of a day. Donati still hadn't shown up when I left." He ran his hand through his hair.

"That does sound like a waste," I said. I brought my steaming mug to my mouth and blew, trying to cool off the hot liquid. "I would never have let that happen," I said absentmindedly. I took a sip and cringed as it ran down my throat.

"Yeah - if only," he said.

I brought my mug back down to the counter and tilted my head in thought. What if? I thought about the idea of working for the District Attorney's office. I knew I didn't want to be a defense attorney any more. Aside from being a lawyer I wasn't sure what else I would be good at career-wise. Putting away the bad guys instead of defending them seemed like the perfect solution to my conundrum.

The following day I made an appointment to speak to District Attorney James Ferguson. After much consideration, and a lot of determination on my part, I was assigned a new role as Assistant District Attorney.

Wanting to make a clean, fresh start Lucas and I hired people to clean out my apartment. I donated or got rid of everything, with the exception of clothes. Lucas and I had time before we began our new jobs, so going to the beach house was the perfect solution.

I was sleeping better and my confidence was returning. The memories of what had happened the few months before lingered in dreams but had become less and less frequent. Lucas was a solid, constant fixture in my life. We had been brought together by chance and were now bound by circumstances.

I stood up and stretched, feeling sun-soaked and wind-blown. Lucas was making his way back towards the house; it was getting close to dinner time. I went into the kitchen and opened the door to the fridge, staring blankly at its contents. Lucas came in, breathing heavily.

"Hey," he said.

"Hey," I replied.

He came up behind me, gave my backside a soft squeeze, and reached in for bottled water. I giggled at his gesture and gave his damp shoulder a swat. He drank his water with a smile on his face.

"How was the run?"

He stopped drinking and caught his breath. "It was good. Hot."

"How about steaks for dinner? You feel like grilling?"

"Sure. Just let me shower. I'll be out in a few."

He disappeared and I began prepping a salad to have with the steaks. I pulled out lettuce, tomatoes, a cucumber and red pepper. I had finished rinsing everything and was chopping tomatoes when Lucas came back into the kitchen. I glanced over my shoulder at him and reveled in his appearance. He wore nothing but cargo shorts. Water dripped from the dark curls around his neck and he smelled fresh and clean. I licked then bit my bottom lip, secretly pleased that he hadn't shaved. I looked back to what I was doing.

"Hey, you want a beer?" he asked.

"Sure."

I heard the clinking of bottles and looked up to see him close the door with his hip; plate of steaks in one hand, two beer bottles in the other. He put a bottle on the counter next to me and kissed my temple. I closed my eyes, loving the feel of stubble against my skin.

"I'm gonna head out and start the grill."

"Okay, I'm almost finished here," I said, opening my beer. "I'll be out when I'm done."

When I was done putting the salad together, I headed out to join Lucas on the back deck. On my way out I noticed my laptop on the kitchen table and decided to check my email. Since I had been involved in reading my mother's journals for the past few days, I had let my world in New York fall by the wayside.

The grill was smoking with delicious aromas from the steaks. The sun was beginning to go down, setting the sky off with hues of pinks and purples. The air was cool and salty. I sat in an Adirondack chair in the shade and took a big pull of my beer. The bubbles made me burp and I giggled.

"You can't stand to just enjoy yourself, can you?" Lucas asked.

"It's not work," I said defensively. "I'm just going to see what's going on in the world."

"We have a little more than a week left. The world can wait if you ask me," he said finishing his beer. He held up his empty bottle. "I'm going in for another. You need one?"

"No thanks."

Lucas disappeared into the house as I logged into my email. I had eighty unread messages, which I thought was a conservative number considering how long it had been. I scanned through them, deleting the ads and other unimportant things. I got to the end of the list and sat up straight in my chair with a gasp. Lucas was just coming back out and he was next to me at once.

"What? Jen, what is it?"

I looked up at him, gaping. I couldn't find words so I just pointed. He squinted as he turned his attention from my face to the computer screen. "Oh shit."

I looked back to my screen and opened the email.

From: Thomas Hawthorne
Subject: Hope you are well
Date: August 6 2012 01:27
To: Jennifer Callahan

Dear Jennifer,

I'm sorry it has taken me so long to be in contact. I was detained, briefly, but am now free to catch up on unfinished business.

I send my condolences for the death of your father. It was unfortunate what happened and I apologize I couldn't have been there for you. I so look forward to seeing you again soon. I've been eager to continue what we started in California and will be anxious to hear from you.

Please let me know if there is anything at all that you need. I will be in New York until the end of the week and then will be heading back to California. I'm here for you now so don't hesitate to call or write. Until then, take care.

Sincerest regards,
Thomas Hawthorne
COO, Wallace Enterprises

It was silent for a long time between Lucas and me. I wondered what he was thinking and if it mirrored my own thoughts, because I was reeling. The words 'free now' resonated over and over in my mind. He wasn't in jail but out in the world and free to do what he wanted. How could this be? Thomas was delusional. He actually thought something was going on between us and I needed him. It was absurd. I looked to Lucas for some clarity. Only he didn't look clear-headed. He looked angry. His eyebrows were pushed tightly together, the lines in-between prominent. His jaw was clenched and his lips were set in a thin line. Oh shit.

I stood up and put my laptop down on the chair. I touched his arm but he turned away from me, pretending to be suddenly busy with the grill and its contents.

"How is he out?" My voice broke, giving away how scared I felt.

After he had flipped the steaks he put the tongs down and took a long pull from his beer. "I'm not sure." I could tell he was annoyed. "What exactly happened in California?" he asked. "Is there something I should know?"

"Lucas, no! This guy is out of his mind insane! I had dinner with him - one time - and that was only to pump him for information." I began pacing back and forth across the deck. "I don't know what is going through this guy's mind but I don't like it. I don't like it one bit."

Lucas took me by the arm and pulled me into a tight embrace. I was scared all over again. Just when I was beginning to relax and had stopped looking over my shoulder, I get a message from Thomas Hawthorne.

"There shouldn't be anything to worry about," Lucas said.

I pulled out of his embrace and stared at him in disbelief. "Are you kidding me?"

"Look, I know everything that happened - I was there, remember? But this Hawthorne guy is harmless. He's about as scary as a mouse."

"Maybe to you. But I don't like rodents." I was angry. How could this have happened? I stomped into the house and began searching for my phone.

"Where are you going?"

"I'm going to call Sergeant Brentzel. I want to know what the hell is going on and why Thomas was released." I was throwing pillows off the couch, pushing things around on the kitchen table, unable to find my phone.

"Will you calm down please?" Lucas had me by the shoulders and he shook me a little. My fortitude hit a wall and I blinked in surprise. "Calm down."

I met his eyes. "Don't you want to know what's going on?"

"Of course I do." He took me by the elbow and sat me down on the couch. I put my head in my hands. He sat down next to me. "I don't think we should jump to any conclusions."

I sat back and sighed heavily. I wanted to believe that Thomas was harmless and I was just over-reacting. But everything I had been through and all that had happened was still clear in my mind. It was all fresh again and I was scared.

"Thomas Hawthorne didn't play a big part in anything that happened, Jen."

"That we know of," I said. "What about...what about my sis... Gabriella?"

We sat silently for a few moments. I was reeling, trying to find answers to a question that had brought back the past I had almost succeeded in pushing to the back of my mind.

"You call Sarge. I'll go get the steaks." He touched my shoulder gently as he stood up. He held out his cell phone to me.

I wasn't sure if I was ready but I placed the call anyway. I sat back and twirled my hair as I heard the second ring.

"Sergeant Brentzel"

"Hey…Sergeant Brentzel…this is Jennifer Monroe…" I wasn't sure where to begin.

"Hey there Jen. So, you decided to take your dads last name—I think he would have liked that. So…how are things at the beach?"

"They were good…until a few minutes ago." I stood up and began pacing. "I received an email from Thomas Hawthorne a few days ago. I haven't been checking my mail regularly so I just read it."

"Oh…yeah…I wanted to tell you both but I decided to wait until you got back. I didn't want to interrupt your vacation and all. There's really nothing to be worried about."

"Nothing to worry about? Would you like to explain to me why in hell he was released?"

"We didn't have anything solid to hold him on. His lawyer got everything he said in the interview room thrown out. And since that happened we weren't able to obtain any warrants for his hotel."

"What about California? That's where all the evidence is."

"That's out of our jurisdiction, you know that."

I clenched my jaw. "Yes, I understand that. But what about Vance Wallace and the fact that his business ran to California? Don't tell me you couldn't make that stick too?"

There was silence on the other end for a moment. I knew he was probably just as frustrated as I was, maybe even more so. He had been working on the Vance Wallace case for three years. Just because Wallace was dead didn't mean the business aspect of him was finished as well.

"We tried our best to get the evidence that would keep Hawthorne in jail. His lawyer was too good and too quick."

I stopped pacing and squeezed the bridge of my nose. I wanted to scream.

"We haven't put the case to rest yet. It's still open and we plan to clean up the mess Wallace made."

"Well, I plan to make that my first priority when I get back and begin work at the DA's office. There's no way I want Thomas Hawthorne or Vance Wallace getting away with all the shit they've done."

Lucas came in and placed the plate with the cooked steaks on the dining room table.

"I'll be in touch with you." I said and hung up.

I knew when I got back to New York I was going to make things right again. I was going to fight to make the man who started all of this pay once and for all; the man who had started a drug business, who had killed Lucas's parents and mine as well, who had changed my life forever. I didn't care how long it took me but I was going to break apart everything Vance Wallace had built. Thomas Hawthorne was part of it and he was the starting point.

I leaned forward and put my palm on Lucas's cheek. It was warm from the sun. I felt the soft stubble of his beard and leaned in to kiss his lips. "Let's eat."

Coming Soon

an excerpt
from

Untangled Lies

As I walked around the huge penthouse, I admired all of the things money could buy. There was leather furniture, crystal behind the bar and the view—that was priceless. I wandered over to the windows and looked out over the city before me and wondered would I be able to live here? Would I be able to make this place my home and work as my father had? I turned around and leaned against the cold window and imagined my life as a high powered business woman. Designer suits, shoes and handbags, vacations anywhere in the world, parties. It was a lifestyle that was opposite of what I'd been living. My life had been so boring and monotonous. But what about Lucas? The rational side of me was sneaking in and reminding me that my life was no longer boring—I had fallen in love with a sexy, energetic man who brought meaning back into my boring existence.

I heard my cell phone ring and I grabbed it from my purse.

"Hello?"

"Hey hon. You leave work yet?" Lucas said cheerily.

I started to pace around the room as I tried to figure out what time it was back in New York. If it was 2:36 in L.A., then it was almost six in New York. "Yeah, I left already. How's Boston?" I wanted to change the subject fast.

"Eh, it's alright I guess. We're about to head out to a bar…grab a bite and a beer. Or should I say beeyah." He laughed at his attempt at a Boston accent. "What are you up to tonight?"

"Oh, I don't know. I'm just fiddling around. Haven't decided on anything yet." I sat on the bench at the foot of the bed and started twirling my hair.

"Well, text me if you go out, okay? I just want to know you're safe."

I squeezed my eyes shut and put a fist to my forehead. I already was 'out'. In-another-state-out. Suddenly I heard chimes coming from the living room. Was that a doorbell?

"Jen…are you there? Did you hear me?" Lucas sounded nervous.

"Yes, I heard you. I don't have any plans but if I make any I'll let you know, okay? Don't worry about me. You enjoy yourself and I'll see you

189

in a couple of days." As much as I didn't want to get off the phone with him I was anxious that someone was at the door. In fact I was sure of it, because I heard the chimes again. "Hey, you know what? I think I'm gonna take a bath. So I'll let you go and I'll talk to you tomorrow, okay?"

"A bath? You? You hate baths."

"Yeah, well, it's been a long week. I could use a hot soak. That run last night really killed my legs."

"Alright, well, don't drown. I'll call you tomorrow."

"Okay, have a good night."

"I love you."

"I love you too."

I dropped my phone back into my purse then rushed to the door and opened it to see Thomas halfway down the hallway walking to the elevators. He turned at the sound of the door opening.

"Oh, you are here. I thought maybe you hadn't arrived yet. Is everything alright?"

"Yeah, sorry. I was on the balcony and wasn't sure the chimes were actually a doorbell." I laughed and stepped aside. "Come in."

He stepped in and turned to face me. He embraced me tightly and breathed in with his nose in my hair. I stiffened but reciprocated his hug lightly then pulled away.

"This room is really way too much Thomas. It's incredibly unnecessary. I could have stayed in a regular room. I'll only be here for one night and I hate to…"

"One night?" His eyebrows pushed together in confusion. "I was under the impression this was a vacation. One night certainly doesn't constitute much rest and relaxation."

"Yes, well, I have to get back to work. And with the time difference I'll need a night to recoup and get back on New York time. You understand, right?"

He nodded after considering my excuse. "I suppose that's true." He turned around and pointed to the bar. "I'll make us a drink. What'll you have?"

"Scotch rocks, please."

He walked to the bar and I sat on one of the stools. He poured two glasses of scotch and slid one to me. He held up his glass. "To us."

I clinked his glass and took a sip. It was early in L.A. to be drinking but not by my internal clock.

"I'm so glad you changed your mind and decided to come. I'm both surprised and glad."

I looked down at my glass as I spun it around in circles, feeling uneasy for having just lied to Lucas. I wasn't sure what to say to Thomas.

"You know" he said, breaking my thoughts. "When I lived in New York and was in Law school, my parents were taking a bus to see me from Illinois—that's where I grew up. We didn't have much...well, much of anything really. My parents worked hard and struggled to get me into the best schools. On their way to visit me, their bus crashed and they were both killed."

His voice was flat and monotone and he had a distant and empty stare. He began wringing his hands that were resting on the bar in between us. I instinctively reached over and touched them and his eyes, wide with surprise, met mine.

"I'm so sorry that happened. I had no idea."

"I don't know why I just told you that. After what happened to your father I wanted you to know that I understand what it feels like...to lose someone I mean."

I sat back in my chair, taking in all Thomas had just said. I sipped my drink wondering if he was fucking with me. I looked around the room again and realized the money, the power; maybe it was because he grew up with nothing—except loving parents who were willing to do whatever it took to make his dreams come true.

"So...what shall we do this evening, hmm?" he asked, quickly changing the subject

"I haven't really thought about it, actually."

"I thought we could have dinner tonight...for starters." He watched me over the top of his glass while he took a sip.

"I thought maybe you could give me a tour of your business. I mean, I came all the way out here to see what it is that you do. Maybe you could entice me to leave my job in New York after all."

Maybe it was the Scotch making me feel bold. His eyebrows shot up and he tilted his head to the side.

"Oh really? I have to say, Jennifer. You really have done a one-eighty since the last time I talked to you. I can't help but be skeptical."

Oh shit. Be cool. Keep calm. I took another sip of my drink and crossed my legs, trying to seem comfortable. I was anything but.

"As you know, I grew up with money all my life. My father did well and it meant I had the best of things. But this," I turned and waved my hand around the room. "This is impressive. You have a private jet and can afford limousines and penthouse hotel rooms. All of this money you're throwing around has really piqued my interest." I shrugged a shoulder and looked into my lap, trying to seem embarrassed. "I don't know…maybe I wouldn't mind making a little extra money." I looked up and met his eyes. "Is that so bad?"

He put his glass down and steepled his fingers in front of his nose. He was sizing me up, I could tell. He wasn't sure whether or not to trust me. I placed my glass down in front of me and traced the top if it with a finger, circling the crystal slowly.

"You know Thomas; it made me angry when you said you knew about me living with Lucas. I don't like the idea of being watched and followed. It makes me feel like I can't trust you. And I want to trust you, I really do." I looked up and met his eyes. "I came out here on a leap of faith, hoping maybe I could see in you what my father did."

"I'd like to think your father and I had a good relationship. I had great respect for him." He reached across the bar and took one of my hands. He stroked the back of it with his thumb.

I looked down. The talk of my father caused a sting to my heart. I felt a squeeze to my hand. I looked up into Thomas's eyes. They were sparkling with desire. He looked different to me. He seemed genuine and real. Not the smooth-talking snake I had seen all the times before. He released my hand and walked around the bar, turning my stool so it was facing him, and he braced his hands on the arm rests. His nose was inches from mine and I could smell the Scotch on his breath. My breathing picked up and my stomach swelled with butterflies.

"I want to take care of you Jennifer. I want to give you the world."

He leaned in closer, never taking his eyes off mine. He touched his lips lightly to mine and he closed his eyes briefly. He kissed my cheek softly and moved down, kissing until he reached my neck. He put his lips against my ear and whispered, "I can give you anything you desire." I closed my eyes and felt my heart pounding in my chest. He kissed my temple, then the tip of my nose. Our eyes met again and he placed a hand at the back of my neck.

"Thomas…"

"Shhh…"

Acknowledgements

Thank you to my husband who believed in me from day one. All it took was for me to say I think I could write a book.

To my writer's group: Noelle Granger, Bob Byrd, Sandy Gottlieb, Denis Dubay, and Elizabeth Calwell. Your suggestions and comments made a great impact on my writing.

To my editor, Alison Williams: your dedication and support gave me the diligence to work as hard as I did. I am forever grateful to have you as a colleague.

To Elizabeth Hein: thank you for trusting in my work. Your support came when I needed it the most and I will never forget it.

To Jaime Lackey: thank you for taking the best pictures and making the art of jacket cover creation fun.

To Laura Payne: saving the best for last, thank you to my best friend and number one fan. Thank you for your encouragement and unwavering support. Thank you for all of your proofreading, suggestions, and comments. You kept me going every time I wanted to quit. You were never too busy when I was stuck and needed help. This book belongs to you as much as it does to me. God bless you, my dear friend.

About The Author

Rebecca Rose grew up in upstate New York. After marrying her husband, she moved to North Carolina. For five years she worked for Farm Bureau Insurance company. It wasn't until her first child that she decided she no longer wanted to work, but would rather stay home and raise her children.

Several years later she bought her first laptop and decided to write her first novel. She joined a writing critique group, which is where she began writing the novel, Twisted Memories. It was a suggestion from a member that inspired her to continue the story into a series. The second book, Untangled Lies, preceeds the final book, Bonded Love.

Rebecca lives in Holly Springs with her husband and two children and continues to write.

www.ingramcontent.com/pod-product-compliance
Lightning Source LLC
Chambersburg PA
CBHW051511170626
46811CB00002B/753

* 9 7 8 0 9 9 1 1 1 8 5 2 6 *